Also available from Vintage

PARTISANS

AT PLAY IN THE FIELDS OF THE LORD

PETER MATTHIESSEN

Raditzer

VINTAGE BOOKS

A DIVISION OF RANDOM HOUSE · NEW YORK

First Vintage Books Edition, August 1987

Library of Congress Cataloging-in-Publication Data
Matthiessen, Peter.
Raditzer.
I. Title.
PS3563.A8584R3 1987 813'.54   86-40558
ISBN 0-394-75343-7

Manufactured in the United States of America
10 9 8 7 6 5 4 3 2 1

To
S *&* **D**
with love

Raditzer

I

In San Francisco, late on an October afternoon of 1944, the U.S.S. *General Pendleton* was warped out of her berth by a black tug. The men crowding her rails watched an anonymous crewman on the tug's stern. He kept his back to the troopship, hands in pockets, ill at ease beneath their eyes. In a while he shuffled forward and took shelter in the pilot house.

The tug blasted its horn, and at the pier end a starved gull with a dragging wing edged out from behind a bollard. Two others, wings spread, beaks wide, swooped in to punish it, and it fell forward on its dirty breast. It struggled free again, and the two clean gulls, like warders, moved in haughtily and flanked it. The doomed bird huddled where it was, and together the three awaited the next instinct, silently, ceremonially, feathers stirring in the famished wind.

The *Pendleton* creaked heavily on the pilings, washed of her harbor scum by the tug's foam. Then she floated free. With a drumming that shook the ship, the screws churned out of reverse, boiling the foul water beneath the stern. The pier drifted off, and the tug, cast free, swirled eastward toward the cities of the bay. Her whistle unanswered, the *Pendleton* trudged down across a roadstead blotched with wind streaks and oily currents toward the Golden Gate. A buoy rolled upon the tide like a black drunken bishop, its bell—*d-ding-derng*—vague on the cold air.

There would be no convoy, and to the men aboard her the ship seemed fugitive and small. She was gray and slow, rusty with war's neglect, and the landing craft lashed across her foredeck gave her a blunt, cantankerous look, like some old cattle tramp bound outward for Patagonia. In her wake yawped sullen gulls, hell bent on scraps, and dead ahead the great bridge silhouette, eclipsing a pale sun, hung sharp black on a luminous yellow sky. As the ship crept toward it, the arc of the bridge climbed higher and higher, like the jaw of a trap. A storm front, framed in the mighty portal, bruised the ocean distance to the westward.

Now hear this. Now hear this—

The loudspeaker echoed dismally as the bridge soared overhead, engulfing the human cargo milling on the foredeck. The men gaped upward in awe at the red girders, on the spine of which invisible civilian cars ran antlike toward the lights of home. Above the sluggish turbines of the troopship their passage was inaudible.

—Following report immediately to the Officer of the Deck: Abrams, Gioncarlo, Stark, Maloney, Payne, Raditzer, J. Williams—

The *Pendleton* shuddered in a narrow rip where the outgoing tide collided with damp onshore winds. The engines were badly synchronized and the ship was old, and the vibration gradually increased as the Golden Gate fell astern and the long seas of the Pacific tried the hull. A scattering of raindrops shivered on the metal deck plates, and a dark pennant flying from the mast cracked, fluttered, cracked again.

—Raditzer, repeat, Raditzer, report to the O.D. office on the double. Raditzer, repeat, Raditzer—

Before nightfall the Farallon Islands faded and the white wake fell away into oblivion. The gulls which had trailed the ship from shore wheeled fitfully or fled back to the land on darkening wings, and as the coast sank beneath the sea the men shifted one by one to stare ahead. Many had never beheld the open ocean, and few liked what they saw. The western horizon, a strange bright band of light beneath the shades of storm, was wild and ominous. Slowly, retreating backward, the men gathered at the fo'c'sle hatch and went below, leaving one sailor at the rail alone.

Charles Stark was a big man, with the big nose of a prophet in a generous face. His high forehead, not quite balding, made him look older than he was. At this moment, leaning into the wind, he wore his sailor cap upside down and inside out, to keep it from blowing away. His general appearance, while in no way unclean, suggested a man who goes through life incorrigibly rumpled.

Hey Sailor

—the hollow voice of the public-address system boomed down upon him from the bridge—

Square that cap.

Without haste, Stark raised his hands and rearranged the cap upon his forehead. Before lowering them again, he turned up the collar of his pea jacket. His hands were cold from the cable of the rail, and he shoved them into his pockets.

There was something disturbing about putting to sea at dusk, Stark thought, to account for his own forebodings. Standing there, he was struck by the weight of this new experience—he was going to war.

How strange, he thought, how very strange. He thought again of his wife, Charlotte, and gazed toward the land. Below, the ocean surged against the hull.

In a while he turned and observed the hatch, a narrow upright structure like a lightless sentry box in the middle of the foredeck. Stark belonged to a detachment of the human cargo assigned to fire watch around the clock, and this area of the deck, from the base of the superstructure to the bow, would be his station from midnight until four in the morning of each day at sea. The man at this station was also responsible for the operation of the fo'c'sle hatch, which could be opened only from the outside by means of a mighty iron latch. The hatch itself was a heavy door, the base of which was flush with the top step of a ladder leading below. The ladder, inset in the bulkhead, was invisible from above, so that the hatch seemed to open onto a black hole dropping down into the darkness. From this hole issued, as Stark approached, a draft of bad air tainted with human sickness.

Stark made his way down into the troop holds, moving slowly along dim companionways of steel lit here and there by yellow bulbs, then down more ladders, through more holds, tracing the myriad arrows, signs, and numbers, the red hieroglyphics of war, which made it possible for Stark and the others to understand where they were going, though not why.

The signs reflected such a low opinion of their intelligence that Stark wondered how the government could possibly hope to win the war at all.

He entered the latrine and contemplated with distaste the long urinal, like an animal trough, and the grim open stalls. The latrine, embodying the enlisted man's debasement, worked hand in glove with that hollow presence, the public-address system—how pointless that had been, he thought, to order a man alone on a ship's foredeck to rearrange his idiotic cap. Stark took a pencil from his pocket and drew an inscription of his own among the official notices on the wall.

ENLISTED MEN ARE FORBIDDEN
TO DRINK OUT OF THE URINALS

Admiring his handiwork, he was mildly surprised by his own childishness—he had never indulged in *graffiti* in his life. At the same time he was pleased by the nice distinction in the message.

He went on, descending. His own compartment was three decks down, and there was still another deck below. The compartments on each deck were all adjoining, like great pens in a stockyard, and opened one into another through narrow archways set into the bulkheads above the floor. In each compartment the tiers of berths, thin strips of canvas taut between iron rods, were stacked four high, and so close together that a man could not sit up, could only stare blankly at the canvas bulge of the body above him, inches from his face. Because the aisles between bunks were narrow and cluttered, there was no place to stand except in the latrine, which the effects of the ship's motion on the men soon rendered uninhabitable. Thus the men lay prostrate until their turn should come to troop aft to the galley.

Stark had seen the galley, which was much too small. It would be in operation day and night, and the distortion of time in the uncertain meal hours, with the drab light in the cramped confines of the hold, the vibration, the palsied shuddering of the ship, the smell, contributed much to the unhappiness evident in the drawn faces of the men. They were far from home and going farther, going into war. And they were at the mercy of forces beyond their control, not the least of which, especially to those from the inland plains and prairies of America, was the sea rolling silently past above their heads, and but a few inches away on the other side of the throbbing plates.

They lay silently, most of them. A few kept up a pathetic barracks clamor, their words blurred by metallic reverberations, and some huddled, stunned with sickness. The seasick ones, Stark noted, were apt to be the homesick ones, at least at first. Within hours, as the weather worsened, the sickness became general, and the bewildered men retreated into thoughts of home, clutching their pictures and kneading their last letters.

Stark himself did not get seasick, but the bad air dizzied him. Toward ten o'clock he left his bunk and made his way carefully down the ranks to the passages and ladders leading upward. The final ladder to the foredeck mounted into darkness, for the hatch was closed, and it was only by pounding on the inside of the metal door that he made himself heard by the fire watch. There came at last a grating sound, and, a moment after, the hatch flew open, propelling its cursing operator before it.

"Who goes there?"

There was strong wind now, and gusts of rain.

"You my relief?" the fire watch bawled. "I mean who the hell goes there, friend or foe?"

"Foe," Stark said quietly, climbing out.

The man on watch looked fiercely at Stark, then grinned. "Okay, foe. You know the password?"

"Nope. Do you?"

"How would I know the sonofabitch, I never stood no fire watch before." The man wrung out his cap disgustedly. "I'm on the watch for fire, in case you want to know what I'm doin standin around up here half drowned." He slammed the iron door to, and its echo resounded strangely from the iron dungeons beneath their feet.

"Charlie Stark," Stark said, offering his hand. "I saw you in the O. D. office."

In response, the man lunged wildly toward the rail and retched. When he returned he took out a handkerchief and wiped his face. "Don't take it personally," he said. "I'm a country boy name of Jack Gioncarlo, a fightin wop out of Tacoma, Washington. I never been to sea before, and I'm homesick, seasick, and scared half to death. But I'm pleased to meet you, Charlie. You my relief?"

"No," Stark said. "I have the four-to-eight. There's some other guy who's supposed to come on at twelve."

"What's his name?"

"I don't know his name." Stark bent to tie his shoelace. "You seem in pretty good spirits for a guy who's seasick."

"I'm gettin used to it is all. I puked the first time when I seen water between me and the dock, and I ain't hardly had time to catch my breath since." Gioncarlo clung weakly to the latch bar, trying to smile, then winced at the cold rain. "What kind of a outfit they runnin here?" he said after a moment, nodding toward the bridge. "They never issued me no foul weather gear even, Charlie. You get any?"

"No."

"You just like standin around in the rain?"

"I like it better than down below."

"Yeah, I guess so," Gioncarlo said. "We're sure a salty outfit, ain't we? We're goin to foul up the whole Pacific."

This reference to their destination silenced them for a little while, and both probed for cigarettes. The *Pendleton* had begun to roll, and the rain was heavier. Gioncarlo shivered. "Why don't you hole up under the landing craft?" he said. He gestured toward the bulky iron boat that protruded over both port and starboard gunwales. "I could use the company, but you're goin to be out here for four hours yourself."

"Yes," Stark said. "All right."

He slid into the space beneath the boat and, leaning back against its wooden cradle, lit his cigarette. At the flare of the match Gioncarlo bellowed, "Fire!" and laughed dispiritedly. His silhouette, slumped back against the hatch, seemed sadly amorphous in the rain.

Stark, in his seated position, forearms across his knees, slept uneasily, lulled by the ship's motion. But gradually the *Pendleton*'s momentum was challenged by the sea. The long roll of the ship became a blind pitching and yawing, and more and more the slow hulk was stopped short in its plunge into the trough. The impact was marked by a harsh increase in vibration as the great screws, hoisted high on the downward plunge, broke through the surface, and the landing craft creaked and whined in the cold, ill-tempered fits of wind. On the bridge the weak spark of a cigarette moved eerily behind the rain, appearing and disappearing like some uneasy symptom of the ship's agitation.

Gioncarlo, somewhere out of sight, was calling to him. "You think they know where they're goin any more than we do, Charlie?"

"Doesn't feel like it, does it?" Stark said, too quietly to be heard. The glass of the bridge was entirely without light, a precaution against submarines, and the outline of the superstructure swayed unsteadily from side to side as the seas grew. Far below, the sick men would be clutching cold iron berth frames with damp hands—young men courageous and cowardly, intelligent and stupid, unkind and kind, young men renowned or notorious, hated or loved for something by somebody somewhere, now heaped up, emptied, without dignity, individual only in their serial numbers and scars. The true identification marks, Stark thought—a high voice, an idiosyncrasy of step, a comic insight, a gap-toothed grin—were never listed on those files stacked somewhere in the offices behind the dark bridge towering above his head, these offices but outposts in their turn of the higher offices of war.

"I said, Charlie, you think they know where they're goin any better'n we do?"

Stark punched at the hull plates of the landing craft just hard enough to hurt his knuckles.

"Charlie?" Gioncarlo appeared suddenly, stooping beneath the boat. He came forward anxiously in a crouch, hands out to the side, almost falling as the deck canted down and away from him.

"Hello, Jack," Stark said, aware for the first time how very young the boy before him was.

Gioncarlo, on hands and knees, stared in at him, embarrassed, winking the rain from the corners of his eyes. "I just wondered if you knew the time, Charlie, is all," he said. He continued to kneel there, stupefied, until his head lolled and he sank onto his side.

Taking him beneath the arms, Stark dragged him to shelter beneath the landing craft, where he substituted for the boy's wet pea jacket his own dry one. Then he propped Gioncarlo against one of the chocks. Gioncarlo watched him dully, humbly, all defenses leached from his white face.

Ai-ee!—a small shriek whipped away into the wind, like the mortal sound of a land bird blown seaward in the storm. Stark, crouched behind the fo'c'sle hatch, was awakened that same instant by a cold spit of sea which, clearing the bow, sluiced down across the foredeck. He shuddered. Was it he himself who had cried out in his sleep, or was it Gioncarlo? The latter, wild-eyed, fleeing nightmares, came pitching out from beneath the landing craft and would have fallen had Stark not caught him.

"You hear that, Charlie? You hear anything?"

They peered about them.

"What a crazy night!" Gioncarlo tried unsuccessfully to laugh. He stumbled toward the fo'c'sle hatch, extending his arms before him like a blind man, and Stark moved to help him. "That wasn't me made that noise, Charlie. For a second there I thought it was you, maybe fell overboard."

Stark shook his head, uneasy himself, and wrenched the latch bar upward. The hatch swung outward slowly, then very fast, of its own weight. Behind it, the black hole yawned, sighing out its hellish breath as he braced the metal door against the wind and stared.

On the top step of the ladder, at the level of the sill, there rested, as if decapitated, a human head. A hand appeared and clutched the riveted edge of the sill, but its owner made no attempt to haul himself upward into the air, as if in darkness and the stench of human misery he had found matters more to his liking.

Gioncarlo had not seen him. The boy stepped forward, his tense face evidence that he was already breathing through his mouth. At the hatch he hesitated, smiling weakly at Stark, who gestured stupidly at the face on the ladder. The legs of Gioncarlo's trousers were now inches from this face. They served, apparently, as some sort of release for the man in the hole, who at this moment opened his mouth and vomited. Gioncarlo, aware that something terrible was happening to him, turned his eyes downward, squeezed them shut in agony, then stared, appalled, at Stark.

"For the love of God," he croaked. "They're comin up out of their holes and pukin on me." He turned, moaning, and fled toward the rail.

The other man, so far as Stark could see, was totally unaware of Gioncarlo. He continued to stare straight ahead, blinking occasionally, until Stark said, "You all right?"—at which point, gathering up the contents of his mouth, he spat them after the rest. When he made no further effort to help himself, Stark reached down and, with the strength of sudden anger and disgust, hauled the man bodily upward into the open air and stood him upon his feet.

The man was nondescript in size, thin and soft

rather than wiry, as if, all his life, he had eaten sweet, cheap foods. The eyes, aimed straight forward out of a face very wide at the temples and narrow at the chin, were bright, the large ears seemed oddly cocked, and dark hair was matted on his forehead. He touched his arm gingerly where Stark had seized him. Then he wiped his nose and mouth with his sleeve and wiped the sleeve in its turn upon his denims.

"What did you want to go and do that for, mate?" he complained, unwilling to look Stark in the face.

"You feeling better now?" Stark asked him. He spoke solicitously, for in fact he had been surprised by the violence of his own action and felt remorseful.

"You didn't have to go and do it rough like that, mate," the man continued in a voice that was almost singsong in its nagging quality. "A fella bein sick as a dog and all, know what I mean? I mean, it ain't as if you were on the job or nothin—I been behind that door for more'n a hour, and you didn't get around to openin up for a fella, and me poundin and all and screechin." He cocked his head. "Like, if I had happened to been a officer now, you'd find yourself on report, ain't that right, mate?"

Stark did not explain that the wind and sea had muffled any clamor the man might have made, and that he had been dragged out of the hole because he seemed incapable of helping himself. Stark simply stared. And when the man extended his hand he took it.

"Okay," the man said, clinging to Stark an extra second by way of emphasis. "I ain't hard to get along with. All you got to do, mate, is treat me right, see what I mean?"

Abruptly Stark withdrew his hand, and the man shrugged and moved weakly after Gioncarlo. Though the expanse of empty rail was wide, he selected a spot right at the latter's shoulder. Gioncarlo stepped back and glared at him, then said something violent which Stark could not hear, pointing furiously at his own shoes. The man paused long enough to give Gioncarlo the same sidelong, reproachful look he had given Stark and then was sick. Gioncarlo, for Stark's benefit, shook his fist at the back of the man's head before returning to the hatch.

"How about that!" he howled. "He didn't even say he was sorry!"

"I don't think he even knows he did it," Stark said. He watched with morbid fascination the figure clinging to the cables of the rail.

"And then he comes sneakin up and starts rubbin shoulders, and upwind of me, at that. I swear, I don't know why I didn't throw him overboard. I mean it, Charlie, I never seen such a guy before." Gioncarlo, beside himself, was drawing his fouled pants against a ventilator, but gave up suddenly with an outcry of disgust. "I mean, where do you think he dug up grub like this, that's what I want to know. I mean, *I* ate in the galley, and I sure didn't eat nothin could make *this* kind of mess!" He laughed angrily, half-crying in exasperation, and Stark, who had tried to look sympathetic, burst out laughing himself.

"I just don't get it," Gioncarlo said. "I just don't see how a guy like that ever got in the Navy in the first place, Charlie. If that's the kind of a guy they're sendin out to save poor old America, then we're even in a worse shape than I thought."

The man was coming toward them, stretching long fingers toward the metal plates as the deck came up at him, hung suspended for a moment, and fell away again.

"Hi, fellas," he said. His tone invited sympathy for his sufferings.

"Look what you done to my pants and shoes," Gioncarlo said.

"I wouldn't have done it if I knowed it was you, mate," the man said, winking at Stark and attempting to nudge him with his elbow.

"How about sayin you're sorry?" the boy persisted. "You ain't got very good manners, is all I can say."

"No, that's right, fella, I ain't," the man said in a

different tone, gazing at Stark as if Gioncarlo was of no importance. "There weren't nobody to teach me none."

"Well, by Christ *I'll* teach you some—" Gioncarlo started, but at a signal from Stark he subsided.

"You're Stark," the man was saying. "Am I right? You're an older guy, you been to college and everything, you got a little wife for yourself already."

Stark swung the hatch door open. "What about it? I mean, how in hell—"

"I keep my ears open. See, a guy like you has got life all figured out. Life was figured out for a guy like you before you was even born hardly. And I was just wonderin how you got yourself in a mess like this, on this old scow with a bunch of punks, is all. You must have screwed up *some*where." Backing into the hatch, he added before Stark could answer, "Now don't get me wrong. I'm an older guy myself, and it took 'em four years to catch up with me before *I* screwed up. So that makes two of us, Stark. You and me got to stick together. He turned to Gioncarlo. "I'm your relief." He spat. "I don't know if I'm up to workin that door though, especially feelin so sick like I do. It's okay for you big fellas, but they shouldn't ought to put a little fella like me on no job like that." He started down the ladder. When his face reached the level of the top rung, he paused and said to Stark, "Like I say, Stark, I feel awful sick. I don't even know that I got the strength to make it up here again, know what I mean?" His head disappeared into the darkness.

"Wait a minute," Gioncarlo shouted after him. "It ain't Stark you're supposed to relieve, it's me. You get the hell back up here, or you're askin for a court martial. Listen, there's a war on, in case you didn't know it. Listen"—Gioncarlo's voice rose when the man did not answer—"what's your goddam name?"

"Raditzer!"

The name, accented on its first syllable, echoed in the metal shaft—RA-ditzer, -ditzer, -ditz . . .

At midnight the man failed to reappear. Gioncarlo was outraged and threatened to report Raditzer then and there, but Stark managed to calm him. He himself stood most of Raditzer's watch. Stark's attitude exasperated Gioncarlo, who was torn between a stubborn refusal to indulge Raditzer and a feeling that he should share in Charlie's burden. He threatened to go to the deck officer about it whether Stark liked it or not. "I mean, who do you think this guy is?" Gioncarlo said. "Your brother?"

"Maybe he's really pretty sick," Stark said. "Maybe he'll show up tomorrow." He sensed, however, that Raditzer would not appear for duty during the trip but would lurk somewhere below until Stark hunted him out or put him on report.

He was unwilling to do either. On the second day

he moved all his gear into a niche among the block-ing timbers of the landing craft, and since he was liv-ing on the foredeck anyway, it seemed unimportant to him that he was there on duty eight hours instead of four. The storm, sprawling and headless, was fol-lowing them westward. The decks were intermittently awash, the maintenance of the fire watch was sense-less, and though he honored his duty with his presence he no longer took it seriously. The first few nights he remained near the hatch, but on the fourth night a sea breaking across the deck seized him up and swept him violently against the rail cables, nearly washing him over the side.

Too frightened to move, he clung to a stanchion a little while, getting his breath, and blinking resentfully in the direction of the bridge. Stark had heard rumors that the whole ship was being run by the handful of men unaffected by the storm. In any case, no deck officer had ventured forward from the superstructure to investigate the night fire watch, and Stark knew that if he had vanished overboard he might have gone un-missed indefinitely.

He crept in under the landing craft and changed his clothes, and did not come out again during his watch on that night or on nights thereafter.

The storm roared on across the dark days unabated, and even the sick who could still make it gave up ex-peditions to the deck in this foul weather. Raditzer excepted, the other men on watch came and went every four hours, but Stark talked at length to no one but Gioncarlo. The latter had formed a dependence on Stark and came and squatted with him sometimes in his shelter, but for the most part Stark was alone.

He exulted in his solitude, in his long days in the wild isolated realm of wind and water. And one night, as time blurred about him, he thought he sensed the wax and wane of his own burning, a rhythm deeper and more inward still than the pulse of blood which filled his heart. This rhythm somehow aligned itself with the blind, mighty risings and declines of tides and winds and seasons, and he felt, as never before, at one with the earth whirling about him, whirling him out and away from the orderly adjustments of his life, including his beloved young wife Charlotte, who was, as his mother had remarked, so suited to him, and his predestined future in his father's Portland law firm, a future as inexorable—and at this moment, as incredible—as death.

Life was figured out for a guy like you before you was even born hardly.

He swore at Raditzer aloud, surprising himself, for, with his life now potentially endangered, his safe destiny seemed something to be desired, and his painting no more than a disturbing pastime. My God, he thought, a pass-time—what a word of defeat that is! No, I am a painter!—and an access of longing for some unnamed freedom caught at him, drove him to his feet, prepared to bear witness to momentous happenings, apocalyptic visions. In this unreal world, on night watch on a ship in storm, he might even hope to hear across the sea wind the whisper of his own swift flight through time, the meanings, meanings, and confront his own mortality in a way less frightening than exalting. And though this did not come about, the effort was so intense that he was afterward aware of having been in a sort of trance and breathed with difficulty.

Then he sank into deep lassitude and wondered

Nonsense.

Nonsense, Charlie, his father, disappointed, had said. *It's not your fault if that knee keeps you out of the service. Nobody can say you haven't tried—to get in there and do your part, I mean.*

And that had been nonsense too, of course, made nonsense by the cliché. He had only wanted to go, to get away. What he wanted to flee, where he wished to go—these questions were much less clear, for his life was pleasant. There was really nothing to rebel against. Perhaps that was part of it, the fatness of it all, the comfortable assumptions, the infallibility of "good family."

And after all, you can get ahead. It's not as if you had to waste your time.

That was part of it too, that headlong need to "get ahead," like an excited horse. Ahead of what, in the end? Of whom? Oneself?

Unable to answer his own questions, and nursing ill-defined resentments, he neglected his first-year courses. He was in college in Portland, where he was older than most of the students and guarded with the rest—those others who, like himself, had for one reason or another remained behind. It was in this period, striking about for something to sustain him, that he chanced on the journals of Paul Gauguin. He seized upon Gauguin's solution, the wild iconoclasm of it, and devoured the reproductions of the paintings. By the time he read, at last, a life of his hero that replaced the South Sea idyll with syphilis and solitude, he had already begun to draw and sketch.

His sketching was only an impulse at first, and a rather secretive impulse at that. Yet he was astonished and encouraged by the facility of his hand—that humble hand he had never noticed until now, the unsung familiar of baseball bats and hunting knives, of tennis racquets, boat tillers, books, and young summer breasts. To explain his enrollment in an art class, he informed his father that painting attracted him more than the law, a statement borne out by the low order of his grades. He pointed out that the law firm already had several young men more deserving than himself, and that it had always seemed unfair to him that such people be displaced through arrant nepotism. He had armed himself with that phrase, "arrant nepotism," but now that it ballooned in the air between them it sounded very foolish. His father, by way of indicating his own opinion, opened his mouth, then closed eyes and mouth simultaneously. Apparently he was unable to gaze upon his great, sloppy get, who stood there before him in dungrees, sneakers untied, chewing nervously on a golf tee. Charlie had wished to make a somewhat bohemian impression, but concluded miserably that his general appearance exposed his immaturity instead.

Why dammit, boy, his father said, recovering himself, *It's all part of the game. You come from a family of lawyers, the best lawyers in this state, and you are therefore eminently qualified—*

I don't see why, with marks like these. I think it's unjust.

I don't care what you think! I don't intend—now listen to me, Charlie! You've been too damned protected, that's all—

That's exactly right, Charlie said. *That's just the point.*

You don't see that justice has its practical limits, his father fumed, shaking off his tormentor by closing his eyes again. *I've been a lawyer all my life, and I've had to learn that. We want to get ahead, we want to*

*help our own, and by God we'll use every advantage
we have. Not that you don't deserve it—I'm putting
this badly—look here, if you start worrying about the
have-nots, you've picked yourself a lifetime job, and
you'll wind up a have-not yourself!*

The attorney's resentment of his ingrate son had
very much upset him, for this fierceness of tone and
attitude did not suit him, and his hands, clenching
and jumping open, betrayed his unhappiness about
the position he had been forced to take. *If one of those
fellows has to make room for you, then by God, he'll
make room for you, and he'll understand why, too,
even if you don't!*

Charlie said, *I thought you people were concerned
with justice.*

*Strictly speaking, we are not concerned with jus-
tice. We are concerned with justice under the law.
Unfortunately there is sometimes a difference.*

I'm beginning to see that, Charlie said, as his
mother, disregarding his father's dismissive gesture,
tripped blandly into the room.

Please speak to your father more carefully, Charles.

As a compromise, it was agreed that he would study
both art and pre-law until a final decision could be
made. This was in 1942. Though his interest in art
flagged somewhat once the truce had been set up, he
persevered, and two years later, in his senior year,

was working regularly in oils. He had undergone a final operation on his knee and had hopes of entering the service.

His mother had been pleased, unofficially at least, with his first sketches, but the paintings themselves, with their growing size and turbulence, alarmed her. A brooding quality, a hint of darkness, increased her mild concern. *Where do you get such sinister ideas, Charlie?* she inquired on a later occasion. *Not, surely, in this sunny house?* But his father, who was biding his time with an exasperating confidence, chided her for taking Charlie's art so seriously. *I know,* she said, *I suppose it's foolish to take seriously anything one doesn't understand.* Clearly, she loved her upstanding spouse, and easily concealed from his piercing legal eye her gentle and therapeutic malice. Charlie had grinned openly, but his mother refused to recognize that this callow person was a party to her subversion —indeed, he wondered at times if she was a party to it herself.

Art is harmless enough as a pastime, her husband observed, rapping out his pipe. *It is only as a profession that it becomes suspicious.* But the attorney was good-natured about the paintings, apparently resigning himself to art as something any decent boy got out of his system, like loose women and fast driving and drink.

What are you talking about? You act as if art—

Now, never mind, Charles, his mother said. *Did I tell you you needed a haircut?*

In those days, it was true, Charlie habitually drove fast, and drank all he could hold and at times more, and took such strenuous advantage of the many unattended girls that he thought so much love must surely addle his brain. So long as he drank he didn't care too much about his inability to serve his country or to resist preying upon the women of those, he accused himself afterward, who were doing his fighting for him. His shame in regard to his own role, far from holding him in check, seemed only to increase his depredations, the need for which mysteriously ceased with the healing of his knee. Soon he could join the Navy, and his self-respect was accompanied by the emergence in his life of Charlotte Sylvester, a student in his History of Art class, who was only nineteen and thought him splendid.

Charlotte had soft dark hair with a strange gleam of auburn in it, and soft wistful eyes, and a cool mouth in a soft young face that could flower in a miraculous sudden smile. Her smoky voice left Charlie, at least, defenseless. Because she kept to herself, at a discreet remove from the gaggle of her sisters, he thought her nicely diffident and serene, and furthermore she much admired Gauguin. By this time Charlie had learned by heart all Gauguin's Polynesian titles, and though there were many he could not translate, he liked to roll them on his tongue, for their soft sounds were like the roll of seashells in Oceania. She thought this in no way foolish of him and in fact announced aloud what had been his secret conviction from the start, that his identification with these phrases was the sign of an inspired sensibility.

Over wine in cellar restaurants, to the tune of "Moonglow," he spoke to her philosophically of love, alluding in a continental manner to the inevitability of their affair. *D'où venons-nous, Que sommes-nous, Où allons-nous,* he mused at one point, repeating drunkenly across the candlelight the mighty Gauguin theme and flushing immediately at his own sententiousness. *What have I done?* he groaned as Charlotte joined her hands in a reverent way upon the table, her lower lip between her teeth. Sighing, she made him translate the title, expound upon it, until suddenly he broke off and she laughed.

Well, anyway, it was his last and maybe best painting, he blurted angrily, and laughed himself.

Où allons-nous, Charles?

God, I wish I hadn't said that. People have been shot for less.

Quoi? *I mean,* comment?

Have you no mercy?

Oh, but Charles! *I think French is so compelling!*

Charlotte had never had a lover, a remarkable circumstance which he admired more than she did.

Her pleasure in his plan for her doomed virginity made a mockery of his crafty overtures, and she was actually more eager than he thought desirable. That is, his idea of her was so romantic that the willingness of this magical creature to know carnally his own tainted person could only seem an unnatural taste to him, if not somehow depraved. What had struck him as most natural in other girls reawakened in him his heritage of dour puritanism. It did not occur to him, not at first, that her abandon bloomed from the sweet confidence that he meant to marry her. Yet it was probably some such instinct, some idea that a vital freedom was already in jeopardy, that caused him to hesitate before telling her one night that he wanted her to go with him to Ensenada, a fishing village on the Baja California coast of Mexico, where they would become lovers.

She nodded, moved, and took his hand, and instantly he was stirred by latent doubts, and felt shamed by her defenselessness. But his time was short, and Gauguin was ever present, waiting to be invoked, and a week later they set off, telling his parents—hers lived in the East—that they were traveling with friends. He also confided in his mother that they planned to marry, expecting her to be shocked, for he thought somehow that if he approved of Charlotte, then his parents must automatically disapprove of her. And though he laughed with pride and pleasure at his mother's delight—*We think she's* such *a sweet, pretty child, and so very* suitable, *too,* his mother called after him as he fled—Charlotte herself was momentarily diminished in his eyes. The trip itself was a happy one, however, and a few days after they returned, and a few days before he entered the service, he awoke one fine morning feeling infinitely older and realized that he was married.

II

"Raditzer's the name. Remember me?"

At Pearl Harbor, at the replacement center, Stark
had applied for sea duty and been refused on the
grounds of his weak knee. He watched, not without
bitterness, the assignment to sea of the very men who
had been most ill on the voyage from California, including many who had applied for shore stations. Jack
Gioncarlo had also been refused, owing to some afflic-
tion of the inner ear, and—inevitably, Stark felt, as if
the three of them had been fatefully linked by the
episode on the *Pendleton*'s foredeck—they were accompanied in their shame by Raditzer, who inter-

preted his assignment ashore as the fruit of his own cunning. Raditzer had been assigned to the mess hall, and Stark and Gioncarlo to the laundry.

"It looks like we done all right for ourselves," Raditzer chattered on, undaunted by Stark's short nod and paying no attention to Gioncarlo, who groaned aloud. Raditzer, unnaturally pale in the lost tropic noon, had accosted them outside the mess hall. Behind them the ranks of metal barracks trailed tiredly into the foothills, the dry craters, and dun clouds caught and hung on the dark peaks of the jagged Koolaus far above. Stark felt a mild vertigo.

"The only beach we'll hit, Stark, is Waikiki. Am I right?"

"Who asked you?" Gioncarlo said. "It so happens Stark and me put in for sea duty."

"You too, Stark?"

"Me too."

"You didn't have to do that, Stark, with that bad knee I heard you got." He shook his head. "As a matter of fact now, Charlie boy"—and at this point, to Stark's intense irritation, he lowered his voice and glanced about him, as if the two of them shared Stark's guilty secret—"you didn't have to be in the service at all, ain't that right? From what Gioncarlo here's been sayin around, you went and had a couple, maybe three, operations on that knee just so's you *could* get in." He put his hands on his hips, a habit with him, and rose once or twice on the balls of his feet. "Just so's you could get to sing the Star-Spangled Banana and go out and maybe die to save your country. Is that what you're tryin to tell me, Charlie?"

"I'm not trying to tell you a goddam thing."

"You got big ears, is your trouble," Gioncarlo interrupted. "Look, who the hell asked you—"

"Well, *I* believe you, Charlie, never mind what the rest of 'em are sayin. It's what your kind of people, I mean with the advantages and all, you call it no-bless oblige, ain't that it?" He turned to Gioncarlo for the first time. "No-bless oblige is somethin you and me wouldn't know nothin about," he said, and his contempt was sincere and self-inclusive.

"Listen, *I* put in for sea duty too, and I ain't had the advantage of a turd!" Gioncarlo, losing his temper, reached out for Raditzer's collar, but Raditzer moved behind Stark as casually as if he were stepping in out of the rain.

"You're only a kid," he said. "What I'm talkin about ain't got nothin to do with guys like us. I'm talkin about no-bless oblige. Charlie knows what I'm talkin about, right, Charlie?"

Still controlling himself, Stark peered grimly into the rapt face lifted too close to his own, searching out the insidious sarcasm he felt had to be there. Incredibly, the man's leering disbelief was meant good-naturedly. There was no sarcasm there at all, but only awed inquiry into the nature of a man who would undergo operations for the privilege of serving his country when an operation to avoid this fate seemed much more sensible, a man who would apply for sea duty, a man who was apparently, by his own choice, an enlisted man rather than an officer.

"You're democratic, like, right, Charlie?" And Raditzer looked genuinely impressed. He could scarcely contain himself, as if at any moment he might clutch at Charlie to make sure his eyes and ears had not deceived him. "You wanted to fight shoulder to shoulder with us little guys, ain't that right?" And he jerked his head in the direction of Gioncarlo, who cursed him.

"I don't look at it that way," Stark said, red in the face and not at all certain how he *did* look at it. On an impulse, before the trip to Ensenada, he had withdrawn his application for officer's training and had joined the Navy as an enlisted man. He could not account for his decision except for a feeling that in the ranks he might expect the sort of new experience that would be denied him as an officer.

For this he was thought by Charlotte, his family, and his friends, however tenderly, a fool. In school he had always been an officer of his class, and his parents saw no reason why he should not be an officer now. *You're a natural leader,* his father said. *That quality shouldn't be wasted.* And Charlotte too, in her own way, was very ambitious for him. *You mustn't always be such a* romantic, *Charlie.*

Charlotte's attitude disappointed him a little, so inconsistent was it with her naïve bohemianism. For example, she was fiercely protective of his wish to paint, and, though the first to laugh at herself, made it clear that she saw him not as Charlie Stark, cheerful and personable son of cheerful and prosperous parents, but as an outcast of a Philistine society, a creature of darkness, of garrets, privation, and gemlike inner flames. She burned with contempt for "bourgeois values," which included in his case the harboring of any notion that he might one day practice law, and yet, unaware of the paradox, saw his service role as that of officer and gentleman. *You'd be wasting your formal education,* she assured him reasonably. Yet she was chronically unreasonable. She was passionate and petulant, vengeful in small ways and by no means always truthful, and willfully, incorrigibly childish, and he adored her. If she was difficult, she was also so engaging, so marvelously full of life, that her every small gesture enchanted him—yes, and moved him. When she first saw him in his Navy whites she clapped her hands for joy, dancing round and round him. Her former stern position was forgotten. *Oh, you look so I-don't-know-what!* she cried, jumping up into his arms. *With that lovely little behind of yours—I'll miss it so!* And she cried a little while she laughed, her tears as fleeting as light rain on a sunny day.

His family, however, was less taken with the spectacle he presented, his lovely behind notwithstanding, and could scarcely conceal their disappointment. And he knew that his Navy friends, should they ever get wind of the fact that he had had a choice, would call him a moron and worse. Even Gioncarlo, whose parents would have been so deeply proud of a commission, would find it hard to understand. Confronted this way by Raditzer, his decision seemed fatuous to Stark himself, and now Raditzer took advantage of Stark's speechlessness to say, "Just think what you could be doin, forgettin your wife in some officer's club with maybe one of them highballs, a nice rye and ginger ale, and maybe some nice little gook tail on your knee."

"What are you talking about? Look, you don't know me, Raditzer, and I don't know you. So go talk to somebody else, all right?"

"Aw, Charlie, don't get sore now," Raditzer complained. "I was just askin is all. I mean to say, we're only human, ain't that right, Charlie? And after what you done for me on the *Pendleton*, standin watch for a sick buddy and all that, why, you got a friend for life, is all." He seized Stark's hand and pressed it fervently. "Blood brothers," he said. And as if to hide the depth of his emotion Raditzer hurried away, leaving both Stark and Gioncarlo outraged, confused, in doubt, uncomfortable within themselves and with each other.

What are you talking about?

Both Stark and Gioncarlo had wanted sea duty, but their reasons were quite different. Stark had desired the experience of the sea and, potentially, of combat, for motives more personal than patriotic, while Gioncarlo, despite his defensive cynicism, felt that at sea his duty lay, not only to his country but to his family and to all the Italo-Americans, as he referred to them, of Tacoma, Washington. To this end he was quite prepared to undergo the prolonged misery of seasickness which he knew awaited him, and to face the possibility that he might drown or otherwise perish for his pains. Yet his ardor was not puerile, as Stark recognized. A fine man was already taking form within this soft-faced, loud-voiced boy, though as yet Gioncarlo had so little knowledge of, much less respect for, his own perceptions as to ape with enthusiasm the stunted language, postures, practices, and pleasures of the company bullies, mustering contempt only for the queer candor of the shameless Raditzer. His inherent appreciation of the subtle, the meaningful, the humorous, the kind, was equally intense, however, and he had a need to better himself which achieved its most touching expression in his request to Stark, delivered in timidity and anger, that they dine together, at Jack's expense, in a Honolulu restaurant, in order that Stark might teach him proper table manners. Stark had done so quietly, respectfully, talking with lowered eyes under the fierce, frozen gaze of his pupil, who was so self-conscious that he could not chew.

They had survived the experience better friends. Gioncarlo had been raised in poverty, but he boasted of his family quite sincerely, and clearly they were gentle people who had made of Jack a gentle man.

Raditzer, on the other hand, had never had a family or even an address, referring instead to the bars, brothels, and all-night diners of towns up and down the coast as if these well-lit places had been home to him at night, just as the environs of Highway 101, Stark gathered, had been his habitat by day. He seemed to favor the Southern California stretch, a world of wires, lights, shrill billboards, snorting airbrakes, Diesel fumes, fat pastel cars, and gimcrack progress, and he lived there by his wits, a grifter, drifting from outskirts to outskirts, sharp-eyed and quick-fingered, a sort of human magpie. He would proclaim with a frankness not free at all, but constructed for his own torment and that of others, that he was illegitimate, a product of the orphanage. "You know what they put on my birth certificate? Huh? You know what? They put Male Raditzer, that's what, and that's the only name I got." He boasted that he had only himself to look out for, but that nobody had ever looked out for him was so painfully apparent to his listeners that they could not bear to face him in his nakedness or even face one another. Yet, with his hollow voice, raffish air, and ready hand, he maintained a horrid, almost joyful bonhomie, a man-to-man familiarity with hard drink and lurid fornication, to which his most striking contribution was a stale obscenity, unrelieved by either gusto or invention, and vented with a death-defying snigger, wink, and nudge, which delivered all of womankind, including the wives, mothers, and sisters of his audience, to the ranks of some vast unregenerate whoredom. The angry men would listen to him, unable to believe that he would dare suggest to them what in fact he was suggesting—that their wives or girls would surely be unfaithful to them now that they were away at war, if indeed they had not been betrayed already.

"You don't believe me, ask old Charlie Stark there," he said once. "Charlie was home. I bet you had some fun in them years, huh, Charlie?" And because this was true, Stark stood stone-faced, murder in his heart, in the long seconds while the other men observed him.

Raditzer's red ears, like antennae, flared wide in excitement at these moments, his quick eyes reconnoitered, and he displayed an instinct for sidling outward and away from the hatred engendered by his insidiousness that was marvelous to behold. Though popularly considered a parasite and braggart to whom the sole anathema was truth, no precise charge was ever brought against him and, to Stark's mild astonishment, no physical violence was ever wreaked upon his gnomish person. Apparently the other men felt as Stark did, that Raditzer had to be borne with resignation as a creature past help through corrective measures. It seemed unlikely that the man had ever been redeemable since the covert hour of his conception, but had perhaps been placed on earth by a disgruntled God as a kind of latter-day bastard Jesus, an immaculate corruption.

Raditzer himself betrayed small awareness of his singularity and cried out constantly against the perfidy of others. With Stark, however, in a sly, suggestive way, he was more candid—at least it seemed to Stark that a special communication existed between Raditzer and himself. He did not know whether his age, background, and education, distinguishing him in Raditzer's eyes from the other men, accounted for this, or the fact that he had permitted Raditzer his malingerings aboard the *Pendleton*. In any case, true to his word, Raditzer fastened upon Stark as his confidant and friend.

Raditzer unloaded upon Stark the burden of his past, and Stark heard him out, less in sympathy than with bad conscience, a kind of gnawing malaise which as yet he was unable to resolve. It was as if Raditzer were compelling him—and to a certain extent the other men as well—to face what they could not, would not face, a secret self, a specter escaped from the dark attic of the mind. He was the bogeyman in childhood cellars, come back to haunt them, but he was also the wretched troll within, the practitioner of dirty adolescent habits, the latent liar, pervert, coward, suddenly incarnate.

Raditzer always moved too close to Stark, inside his guard, where Charlie could neither hold his eyes nor deal with him as he wished. Raditzer preferred to hover at his shoulder, imperceptibly behind, talking quickly at Stark's ear. He had a habit of holding Stark's arm in a proprietary way, just above the elbow, not in his hand but between his thumb and forefinger.

Long before Stark noticed it, this habit bothered him, and instinctively he would jerk his arm away. Raditzer would then draw back as if he had been warned, but in a little while, persistent as a fly, he would alight again. It was the suspense that got on Charlie's nerves and caused him to notice the phenomenon. After that, suspense became physical distaste—he found himself shrinking from the fingers in advance.

One tropical day, standing on the mess-hall porch

awaiting the noon rains, he became aware of the hovering fingers. He swung his arm back as if he meant to turn, and smashed Raditzer's hand hard on the post of the porch railing. "Sorry," he said. He was genuinely sorry and startled by his own action, but his face and voice were cold.

Raditzer looked at him, then at the hand. The fingers were bunched like the toes of a dead bird, and Raditzer stared at them, on his face that expression of astonishment and shock which, in a child, passes immediately to tears. But he exposed his hurt only for that one moment before reassuming the face he wore before the world. He looked up again, and Charlie could not face him.

This was the strange part of it, that in the very moment he felt pity for Raditzer—a pity inspired, more perplexing still, by Raditzer's rat courage—he felt also horror. Yet the pity was real, a sensation so profound that the pit of his chest seemed to crack and fall away like the floor of a rusty can, leaving him weakly draining in his inability to recompense the man for his terrible disadvantages. Raditzer, prepared for life as he had been, could no more help himself than the carcass of a saint could help its stench.

But the revulsion was there too, and so far out of control that, had Raditzer touched him again now, he would have recoiled openly, and had Raditzer persisted, he would have smashed him away in a frenzy, like some sort of mantis. A frenzy—he found this hard to believe of himself, but it was true.

"Look, I said I was sorry, and I am."

"I know you, Charlie."

"What does that mean?" Charlie said.

"You know what I mean," Raditzer said. He nodded wisely, hands on his hips, rising and falling on the balls of his feet.

"It ain't like I was born yesterday, am I right, Charlie?" This was his favorite expression, and indeed it was tempting to think that Raditzer was ageless, that he had never been a child at all but was instead a creature who might well have existed throughout the history of man, replacing himself periodically with an exact replica by some unique and terrifying asexual process, a sort of unspeakable budding in far, dark grottoes of the globe.

It was tempting to think this because the reality was so much worse—that Raditzer had once been a small child, identical in his innocence with all the rest of them, and that after two decades of hand-to-mouth survival, his malnutrition, evident in his weak, rickety body, had spread like a cancer to his mind.

In the beginning Stark's dislike was offset by the need to convey to Raditzer some concept of a better world than he had seen. Raditzer's slow-dawning faith—"Well, I got to admit I trust *you*, sometimes, Charlie. And I guess that's somethin, comin from me"—gave Stark an intense pleasure, even stronger than the pleasure he felt in Gioncarlo's dogged intent to improve himself. But sometimes he would wonder whether he himself did not want too badly to believe in the sane world he had inherited, like a trust, from the Stark family, whether the world only seemed civilized because he and the few like him had the money to make it work for them, to avoid being caught up in the wheels.

When Stark read his letters from home the man sat too close to him on the mess-hall porch, spitting into the dust more often and more violently than his chronic catarrh demanded, and uttering observations on the scrofulous nature of mankind which Stark alone among their companions, Raditzer said, was capable of understanding. Raditzer's speech was interesting only in the intensity of its destructiveness. His hatreds were unselective, and his philosophy so shallow that it parodied the cheap credos of his mentors, the radio "personalities" to whom he referred by their first names with the same intimate affection and admiration that men like Gioncarlo reserved for their families. Raditzer listened avidly to the radio, staring at it as if otherwise he might miss something, and his aimless laughter from the far corner of the recreation hall was the loneliest sound Stark had ever heard. There was no amusement in it, only the need to laugh like other men. Indeed he was painfully humorless. It was as if, in the sterile circumstances of his creation, the gene of humor had no place, leaving him bereft of even this last solace.

One day, going to get his mail, Stark saw Raditzer loitering at the corner of the mess hall. Raditzer, imagining himself unobserved, was watching the others open letters. In profile in the shadows, his face looked adolescent. White cap cocked over his left eye, cuffs rolled back on his new tattoos, and a bunch of useless keys and knives slung from the wide belt he affected with his tailor-made bell-bottomed denims, he looked like a little boy playing sailor. His mouth was slack, and his tongue licked nervously at the surface of his lower lip.

Afterward he could not forget the expression on Raditzer's face. He attempted to sketch it in his writing pad, even trying to imagine him as he must have looked as a child, thin-headed and chinless, by the wall of an orphanage yard. It did not work. The characteristic expression of pinched, furtive truculence Raditzer assumed the moment he glimpsed Stark was much too vivid.

"Look at these punks, will you, Charlie? You'd think—"

They went together to get Stark's mail, and

Raditzer strutted in his bell-bottoms, thumbs hooked into his belt. Stark wondered whether the man did not lurk in wait each day so that he might sit with someone on the mess-hall steps and identify in this pathetic way with the news from home.

"There's that old blue letter, Charlie boy."

Raditzer never hinted, as he did with the others, that Stark's wife had by now assuaged her lusts with some civilian. Nevertheless he spoke of her in an offensive way.

"Writin every day like that, she must really have her pants hot for you is all I can say."

"Well, say it in some other way then, will you?"

"Take it easy now. I don't mean nothin personal, Charlie, it's just in a manner of speakin, like. Like a guy might speak of his own mother havin a wild hair up—"

"Dear God—"

"—and not mean *her* exactly, know what I mean?"

Stark laughed harshly, shaking his head, and Raditzer, confused, leered feverishly. At the same time Raditzer glanced around to see if the other men were aware of their conviviality. There was no way of dealing with him short of total rejection, and though Stark knew that his friends disliked his relationship with Raditzer, he was not ready to give in to this temptation. Much as he disliked Raditzer's word choice in juxtaposition with Charlotte's name, he had to admit that Raditzer's attitude conveyed respect for her, and that possibly he himself was being a prig. Since he told Raditzer almost nothing about her, the man imagined a good deal and was constantly conjecturing aloud about some beautiful and mysterious quality of Charlotte unreflected in his own experience with women.

Raditzer's admiration of what he considered Stark's marriage to be—he played with the concept of Charlotte and Charlie as a child might play with imaginary friends—had the disturbing effect of causing Stark to scrutinize it more closely than he would have liked, to face the fact, finally, that even the interlude in Mexico which he remembered so warmly had been marred, at its end, by a seizure of foreboding, doubt

When he came with champagne to the ceremonial room he found her sitting upright on the bed, legs tucked beneath her, head bowed, nude. He gazed at her, feeling indecent fully dressed. She lifted her head after a moment, and her expression said, What do you think of me? Do you love me?

Her candor made him curiously shy, and he made love to her clumsily and hurt her, so that his final cry was less in transport than chagrin. In tears, she told him that nothing so wonderful had ever happened to her, and though he knew this was untrue, at least in the sense she meant him to understand it, he was so touched by her effort to console him that he almost cried himself.

That first night in Ensenada they lay in a high bed, holding hands and staring up at a chalk-white ceiling, listening to the *tequila* drinkers and the guitars in the *cantina* below. In the morning the sun soared from behind the brown plateaus above the village and turned to pink the boat sails and the sand. That day they went back into the hills, to a mysterious country where white boulders ringed a pale, still mountain lake. Three days later, in the afternoon, still damp from the sea, she gave a little moan and bit his shoulder, then pressed her face against his throat and laughed and cried. *It happened! Oh, just think, it happened!* Then, in a rush of shyness, she blushed and closed her eyes, and he contemplated her pure face on the sunlit pillow with more emotion than he had ever known. She smelled faintly of salt water and sunburn lotion—her flesh was still cool where the bathing suit had been—and the tan skin of her soft arm was childlike on the fresh, coarse sheet. He had imagined she might look different now, but if anything she looked more virginal than ever. Though feigning sleep, she knew he watched her, and she was trying not to smile. She drew the sheet up slowly until most of her face was hidden before opening her brown eyes very wide, and he kissed her smiling mouth through the sheet. *I love you, I love you,* he murmured, and there was a funny gurgling response. She felt through their warmth for his hand.

Hello, Char, she whispered. *Hello, Shar,* he said. *Shar and Char,* she said and giggled. *Char and Shar, you mean,* he said. Then she turned her head aside and laughed in a new soft sleepy way.

A little later she said, NOA NOA, *Char.* And when he had kissed her she said, *Char, you see? I've been reading Gauguin too.* When he was silent she said, *Do you know what* NOA NOA *means?*

Yes.

It means something like 'enchantment.'

Yes. He felt a sharp lurch of depression and, pretending to shift position, turned his back on her. Then, feeling he must speak, he asked her if she knew the meaning of MANAO TUPAPAU. *You know,* he said, turning toward her once more, *the one of the young girl lying naked face down on the bed, just the way you are, with the dark figure in the background.*

Yes, she said, after a second's pause. *I know the one.*

It means 'Spirit of the Dead Watching.'

I know, she said, and her eyes filled with tears. Clearly she thought that he referred to the possibility that he might die in combat, but in an odd moment of detachment, though moved by her dismay, he could not bring himself to comfort her.

Char? she said. *Char, you won't find a native girl out there, like your old Gauguin did?*

He took her immediately into his arms and hugged her. He wanted badly to be hugged himself.

Char? Are we really going to get married? Are we?

Oh, darling, of course we are—of course, of course.

But as he lay there his face, reflected in the tilted mirror on the staid bureau, was apprehensive. Under scrutiny, its smile faltered. Framed by her soft hair and small bare shoulders, it stared at him palely, disembodied, as strange to him as a record he once had heard of his own voice. Who are you, the reflection demanded, what are you doing there? He removed his hand from the small of Charlotte's back and waved at the face derisively.

But Char? Are you sure *you want to?*

He nodded vigorously, but the mirror smile faltered again.

His mind wandered to Gauguin's journals, to the beautiful scene in the mountain valley of Punaru, where the painter had watched the naked girl bathing in the spring water. She had sensed his presence and disappeared below the surface.

Quickly I looked into the river—no one, nothing— only an enormous eel which wound in and out among the small stones at the bottom.

The halo of daylight on the glass evaporated, and gradually his face faded. Through the window twilight came, cold as a vapor, and a bright surf of high misshapen clouds, crests still aflame, subsided at last in thin spent grays. A strand of Charlotte's hair strayed on his lips as an outrider of the evening airs searched the still room impatiently, like a bat

"Am I right, Charlie? Huh? Well, am I or ain't I?"

"Yeah, I guess so." He had not been listening.

"*Guess* so? Hell, yes. Why, I seen girls like Charlotte myself, many's and many's the time. Like in the movies. Real class, I mean, ridin around in big convertibles with white teeth and white hair, laughin. Girls like Charlotte are always so kind of white—pure, like, did y'ever notice, Charlie? White as snow. They don't never sweat, they ain't got hair hardly except on their head, it's like they didn't even have no insides, like. This is goin to sound kind of stupid, but I'll tell you somethin about when I was a kid—I never could imagine girls like Charlotte eatin food, let alone in the can, or even in the sack, puttin out for some guy. See, when I was a kid I was always lookin into toy stores, and I noticed like the way them toy animals was always so clean and smooth between the legs. Well, that's the way I always thought of girls like Charlotte. Ain't that stupid, Charlie?"

"I don't know," Stark said. "It's really quite a theory."

Raditzer shook his head mournfully. "Christ, I never known nothin but tramps and whores!"

Stark rarely encouraged Raditzer with an answer. The man did not seem to mind. Between outbursts he would hawk and spit and play with his knife and gaze resentfully about him.

"And that's all these other punks are ever goin to get, don't let 'em tell you different, Charlie boy. I know their kind of women. Why, Christ, the first piece I ever had was the gray-haired mother in one of them foster homes they put me in, and me thirteen. You take Gioncarlo there, moonin around about marryin that dago broad of his, you'd think—"

He stopped short when Stark looked up.

"What I mean is," he went on after a moment, "you and Charlotte now, you don't go in for all this beer and condoms and parked cars—you got class, ain't that right? I mean, am I right or am I wrong?"

Stark shrugged him away, sighing.

"Now you take with Charlotte, love is a thing of beauty, like, kind of a joy forevermore, you might say. She wouldn't cheat on you, huh, Charlie? And you wouldn't go cheatin on her like these other guys do, down in them gook cat-houses in Honolulu, ain't that right, Charlie? Huh? I said, ain't that right, Charlie?"

"I don't suppose so." He gazed down at Raditzer's

hand, which was tugging feverishly at his sleeve. Raditzer withdrew it.

"Hell, no, you wouldn't cheat on Charlotte. Now a guy like Gioncarlo and them others, they don't know no better."

"Oh, nuts." Stark folded his letter and put it in his hip pocket. "I mean, how do you *know* I wouldn't? What makes *me* so goddam different? And you don't know anything about Gioncarlo's girl. I think she sounds just fine."

Stark's tone was colder than he had intended, and Raditzer subsided. This is the way you made me, his injured glance seemed to say whenever he was criticized—you, my unwed parents, the state, the world—and though I am an outcast, you are going to have to live with me, take responsibility for me, carry me, because I will not do my part. He was a sort of ambulatory bad conscience for mankind, Stark once explained to Gioncarlo, with a certain distaste for the overblown phrase as well as for his own indulgent attitude toward Raditzer. Gioncarlo and the other men could not or would not understand this attitude, and he soon gave up trying to account for it. But the guilt he felt in the man's presence was quite real, and he knew that, should the occasion arise, he would allow Raditzer to take advantage of him again. The thing that moved him most—and the reason he would not forsake him—was Raditzer's heartbreaking un-awareness that he had entered the world a pauper, with nothing mental, physical, or spiritual to recommend him.

Nevertheless it was difficult to piece together the dark tale of Raditzer's past, not only because he frequently contradicted himself, but because no single human being could possibly have survived all the shocking experience with which he attempted to regale his ingenuous new friend. "I mean, you ain't seen *nothin,* Charlie," he remarked once, patronizingly. "It's like all your life you been livin in a garden." This was perfectly true, Charlie concluded ruefully, not only of himself but of Charlotte and his family, of most of the people he had known. And certainly Raditzer had known no gardens. In the orphanage, it appeared, he had been smaller and less able than the other children and had set off on the road of life as flunky, punching bag, and prey of apprentice thugs and perverts.

"How's that for a beginning?" he grieved once. "The other kids told me I was the slip-up of some whore and was lucky I didn't wind up in a sewer. I knew what they was talkin about too, and me only eight."

"You didn't believe that, did you?"

"Why not? It ain't like I was the only one in that place, don't you worry."

"And you never saw your mother?" Stark asked, fiddling with his pen. Raditzer had come upon him writing a letter to his parents, and Stark felt vaguely guilty.

"Are you kiddin? Not unless I run into the old slut later on and never known it." Raditzer shivered with resentment. "I remember once I saved up the price of a whore, and another kid with me sayin, Them lousy whores, they was old enough to be our mother. It gave me kind of a funny feelin, know what I mean?"

Charlie nodded in discomfort.

And suddenly Raditzer gave a little screech, his sharp face split open like a burst fruit. "And then I says to myself, shit, I says, that wasn't no fuckin mother love you was after there, you was after a good five-buck ride, and that's what you got, mother or no dirty fuckin mother!" He glared wildly at Charlie. Then he got up and moved away.

Though Stark thought his own interest morbid, he found himself more and more absorbed by Raditzer and drawn to protect the man through an apprehension close to dread. The callus grown of his grinding humiliations led Raditzer to a startling candor, which in his case was by no means the same as being truthful, and this candor, applied to the motives of others, contributed much to his growing unpopularity. His knowing assumptions in regard to his fellows were based on the subterranean half-world which was all he had ever known, and he was therefore incredibly innocent—it was this word, Stark reflected, that finally described him best—not of the darkness, but of the light.

Raditzer was everywhere and nowhere at once, forever on the edge of all activities but never part of them, appearing and disappearing on innumerable little errands which he construed to be to his own advantage. In some obscure executive capacity he had prospered in the mess hall, and within a matter of weeks had gone into partnership with a conclave of local Chinese in the operation of a restaurant in Honolulu. The overhead of this enterprise, Raditzer confided, was considerably reduced by the use of Navy stores for its basic materials.

While the restaurant flourished, the men whom Raditzer looked upon as his friends were invited as his guests, and Stark went once with Gioncarlo. They sat at the best table behind huge exotic drinks called Singapore Slings and listened to songs like "Princess Papooli Has Plenty Papaya" and "The Crazy-Eyed Mare of Kaunakikae." Gioncarlo had at first refused to go, on the grounds that Raditzer was no friend of his and never would be, and that he did not want to be beholden to him. He finally agreed to accompany Stark on condition that he pay for his own meal.

In the end this proved impossible to do. Raditzer, who was there that night, directing the operation from a dark table by the corner of the bar, saw to it that no check was ever presented. His Chinese cronies, self-effacing, allowed Raditzer the limelight, slipping up to him sideways, oblique as twin funeral attendants, from their stations at the door and in the kitchen. Nevertheless Stark guessed that these shy creatures were very much in charge, accepting Raditzer's Western self-advertisement as the price of the raw materials he supplied them at little or no risk to themselves. For Raditzer was incapable of managing this enterprise and was almost certainly the tool of people smarter than himself, whom he imagined he had eating from his hand. And this was perhaps the saddest thing of all—that Raditzer's instinct toward small knavery was unsupported by any talent, that he could not command even that negative respect accorded the successful sharper.

"That miserable little thief—!"

Gioncarlo at last shouted for the check, and Raditzer sent over the singer. She was a large, languorous girl in a tight white dress with a Chinese slit up to the hipbone and a yawning bodice. She had somehow come by bamboo hair and the name of Myrna, and she was instantly familiar to Stark in a way that eluded him, excited him.

"Is everything okay, boys? I'm Myrna, and I'm very happy to meet you social here, I'm sure."

Myrna had been humming when she arrived at the table, and continued to hum when she leaned over to soothe Gioncarlo. The humming seemed abstracted, sad, an outward sign, Stark assured himself drunkenly, of some wistful interior existence in which she took refuge from the vulgarity of her livelihood. He wanted to think of her as a delicate Oriental lotus, but though her general appearance was Oriental, she was scarcely delicate. She had a large mouth and freewheeling breasts and gave off great wafts of jasmine attars, and she smothered Gioncarlo's protests about the check, breathing sweet nothings into his ear and keeping her yearning bosom inches from his nose. He sat stupefied. Stark too was impressed with her breasts, which looked to him quite edible, and amused himself by attempting to discern, way down in the warm cleft, her navel.

Turn a little this way, there's a dear.

No. Yes. Wait—there we are. Whoops. No. No, you are running a little to fat, Myrna. Or perhaps the trouble is I can no longer focus.

And Myrna, please, how do you look from behind?

He watched her walk away. Beneath the coarse silk, her slow, sleepy hips were firm and smooth as giant mushrooms, and he groaned. Unwillingly he thought of Charlotte and of her discreet figure, of the pride she took in that flat, brisk little behind.

"I feel like I been raped," Jack said.

"Me too, and I was only an innocent bystander." Stark shifted in his seat. "For some reason, these damned sailor pants feel too tight for me. You ever have that problem?"

Gioncarlo laughed. "I got it now," he said. "We been out here too long, when something like that looks good to us. I mean, when you get right down to it, she's a mess." He laughed again when Charlie shook his fist at her.

"It's all the wrong things about her that get me," Stark complained, not sure of this at all, and afflicted in his vitals by deeper longings, beyond lust. "All that cruddy perfume and those big dugs and that monster ass." He ground his teeth. "She's made a low, slavering beast of me."

"You're drunk," Gioncarlo said, drunk himself. "She's a goddam mess."

The girl was talking to Raditzer, glancing at them over her shoulder. She winked at Stark, and Raditzer goosed her for their benefit. Raditzer was wearing big dark glasses.

Oo, the bitch. She's sniffed me out.

Raditzer intercepted Stark on his way back from the men's room and asked him what he thought of Myrna.

"Fine, big strapping girl," Stark said. Smiling, he put his hand on Raditzer's shoulder. "Thanks very much for the evening, it's been great."

"She kind of likes you, Charlie." Raditzer nudged him. "It's a good thing you ain't like all the other guys, right, Charlie? Like it ain't every sailor gets a chance at somethin like this. This Heinie ain't no whore neither—that's her real name, Heinie, how do you like that one?—only I changed it to Myrna, see, to give the kid a little class—anyway, she ain't no whore. I guess you're about the only sailor in Honolulu would kick her out of bed, right?"

"Right." Swaying, unable to help himself, he watched the girl at the bar, and she watched him.

Raditzer whistled softly. "I really got to hand it to you, Charlie-boy." He shook his head. "But, on the other hand, this kid ain't your style at all, now, is she? Not when you got that sweet little Charlotte waitin home, huh, Charlie?"

"No, indeed." He started away. "I'll be seeing you, Raditzer. Thanks."

As he passed the girl she shifted around on her stool. She was still humming. "One more for the road, Char-lie?"

"I guess I've had enough, thanks."

"G'night, Char-lie. Come and see me, Char-lie. Maybe we take a walk along beach."

He paused. "Is your name really Heinie, Myrna?"

She shook her head. "Va-*hee*-nay. V-A-H-I-N-E. The boss says it Heinie, but it is Vahine." She shrugged. "My father were a Chinese trader, all through the South Sea island he go with a big bag, very old, smart man. My mother is Hawaiian. He said it was a real Maori name, like in Tahiti. Tahiti is like Hawaiian, only not the same. You know?" She shrugged again. "I don't know."

Stark nodded. The girl's face was still eerily familiar to him. He steadied himself with one hand on the bar, and as her deep eyes widened in concern it came to him—Gauguin's Hivaoa, the dark peaks and pandanus trees, blacks, purples, reds, and fiery yellows, and the face emerged on the fabric of the vision. *Vahine. Vahine*—the word meant girl or woman.

TE ARII VAHINE—which of the canvases was that?

"My father were a nice Chinese man." She was brooding softly, scratching a thick white shoulder. "He sure be a surprise to see his little Vahine workin in this kind of a place." Bewildered, she laughed abruptly. She looked frightened, like a huge, simple child, and he reached over on impulse and stroked her fleshy face once, gently.

"So long, little Vahine," he murmured drunk, grinning contemptuously at his own sentimentality but glad of it when she smiled, and pressed the smile to his flushed cheek.

Then she leaned back and peered into his face and

ran her fingernail lightly across his forehead in a gesture intimate and gentle, a lover's gesture, and asked him softly why it was that, when he smiled, two sad furrows appeared upon his brow, as if at any moment he might cry?

How different had been Charlotte's observation about his face—*It's so marvelously uncomplicated, Char!* How sprightly of his Charlotte that had been —and that villainous adjective described so much about her. How charmingly no-nonsense, how American, he brooded soddenly, by comparison with the freedom, the animal warmth, of this unspoiled native girl who had seen so intuitively the artistic torment raging behind the big-nosed, balding exterior of Charles P. Stark, the weekend Gauguin—this title was Charlotte's comic inspiration too—who even now as he rose to leave before it was too late, let her hand flutter down from his cheek across his chest and stomach.

"Oo, *Char*-lie."

Yes, indeed, Myrn.

VAHINE NO TE VI.

Walking down the street, half-carrying Gioncarlo, Stark laughed at his own fatuousness and could not stop himself. "Lotus," he said and shook his head. "Why, you damn fool!"

"Sonsabitches," Gioncarlo mumbled. "They're all laughin at me."

They were nearing a small park, from the far side of which the buses departed for Pearl Harbor. In the middle of the park a narrow Japanese footbridge crossed a dirty open trench of shallow water, an aborted stream from the mountains behind the city. During the war the trench received a nightly quota of men too drunk to negotiate the bridge. The sides of the trench were slippery and steep, and the fallen were often unable to climb out again. For the shore patrol, they knew, the trench served as a rough gauge of reprehensible drunkenness. The shore patrol inspected its contents periodically during the night and arrested any man found seated in it.

Gioncarlo and Stark reconnoitered it carefully and, after fifteen minutes of tactical preparation and a flanking maneuver or two, crossed the bridge successfully on their hands and knees.

III

Stark kept away from the restaurant for several months despite Raditzer's repeated invitations and a series of inscrutable notes from Myrna which Raditzer, winking, slipped to him like so many dirty pictures. Plainly Raditzer was testing Stark's loyalty to Charlotte, and despite his cajoleries was sincerely pleased that Stark was able to resist. "I got to hand it to you, Charlie-boy, you got real class," Raditzer would say, shaking his head in admiration and inserting his little finger in his ear for a quick scratch, a habit he indulged whenever he felt gleeful.

Through friends in San Francisco, Stark had come

to know some kind people named Adams, who had a big house high above Honolulu, off the road to the Pali Pass, as well as a beach cottage across the island at Punaluu. With the Adamses he could talk of something besides the service and sports and sex, and their island legends he found fascinating. Once he flew with Carter Adams to Maui, where they camped for two days on the great volcano of Haleakala—the Hawaiian name, he was told, meant "mountain of the fighting clouds." At the base Stark had a sketch pad, charcoal pencil, and pastels, but now he also bought a set of paints which he used on liberty and left at the Adams house.

At other times, with Gioncarlo and a friend of theirs named Steve R. Kubichek, he swam in the surf at Waianae and Haleiwa and rode horses in the valleys behind Diamond Head and got genially drunk on the shady terrace of the Halekalani Hotel near Waikiki.

In Europe, the Germans capitulated, and there were rumors of a huge attack to be launched against the Japanese. Stark thought he was glad of this, but he did not really share the elation of the other men. It now seemed certain that his service to his country would be limited to the loading and unloading from harmless round machines the soiled raiments of authentic warriors in transit through the staging center. He applied regularly for sea duty and was regularly turned down, and after a time he ceased to care, retreating into an endless daydream about Charlotte.

He felt closest to Charlotte at Punaluu, where he went alone every chance he had in a car lent by the Adamses. Invariably he would pause at the Pali Pass, high up in the Koolau Range, overlooking the north shore of Oahu. The mountainside falling away below the straight drop from the pass was choked with strange ferns and air plants and the dark spastic trunks of the *ohia-lehua,* with its silk red tropic flowers, and beyond lay the pineapple farms and canefields of Kaneohe Valley and the blue bight of Kaneohe Bay. This was the windward coast, freshened by noon rains and the restless trades, which swept down out of the north-northeast like the cold breath of the sea. From the mountain heights the great dark cloud shadows crept out across the valley toward the sunny shore, and, beyond, the ocean rolled away forever toward the Tropic of Cancer and the continent of home, toward the Golden Gate and Ensenada.

Not that Punaluu was in any way like Ensenada. It was only that an albatross, lifting and falling tirelessly against the trades, could traverse in a straight line the blue fields between one shore and the other, and this link drew Charlotte nearer. Leaving the world behind him on the far side of the mountains, he would descend from the wind tumult of the pass to an Avalon where she walked, awaiting him, with all the endearing wiles and tempers which her pictures only hinted at and which, conjured, suffused him with longing. He remembered her in a white bathing cap at Ensenada, face sparkling with salt water and eyes nearly closed in the ecstasy of her smile, and liked to think that some particle of the sea that had touched her on that distant coast might have traveled since to Punaluu.

Punaluu was as vivid as the setting of a dream, a small community of Japanese fishermen that lay beneath a sharp, dark cliff and faced on a bright lagoon. The huts were scattered, and the beach house itself was almost hidden from the road in a grove of coco palms. Stark had made friends with the Adams's caretaker, a young Japanese fisher named Robert Ariyoshi. Sometimes, when Stark stayed the night, Robert would appear at dawn in the small boat and take him fishing. Robert used the Hawaiian names for the reef fishes with their turgid, bloody colors, for the small silver jack which he called *papio,* and for the barracuda, or *kaku,* of which he was afraid. Floating quietly on the lagoon, the two would see, far out beyond the reefs, the great black forktailed frigate birds, the man-o'-war birds, turning and sweeping on the ocean sky like ancient flying reptiles. Robert called them *mahi-mahi* birds.

Stark went on liberty the night the war was over, and he got as drunk as everybody else. He drank relentlessly all night, not only to salve his own frustrations but because the first excitements of victory had been replaced by bewilderment at the enormity of Hiroshima, and bewilderment by a creeping dread, for innocents had been slaughtered, and on such a scale that motivations were beside the point. Nevertheless the bomb was being hailed as the God-given savior of untold American lives, a kind of mechanical Jesus, he thought, as if its bolt had fallen straight from heaven.

Gott mit uns.

He was with Gioncarlo and several other men but became separated from them around midnight. They had been rolling down the sidewalks, a growing avalanche of white-suited sailors, when the advance was stopped by two members of a Marine shore patrol. A very young submariner had lost his cap and was therefore out of uniform, and one of the marines wanted to arrest him. "Oh, take it easy," the other marine said. "Oh, take it easy," the sailor's friend said, placing his arm around the defendant's shoulders and adjusting his own cap so that it balanced on both tight-pressed heads at once. "Okay, your honor?" He grinned. The sailors and the second marine laughed, and the two boys hobbled forward like children in a three-legged race. "A couple of wise guys," the first marine said. "You're resistin arrest." He stepped forward with his stick and dropped both boys with two neat raps at the base of the skull.

He was a blond puggish youth with protruding lips and cap low over his brow, and he was drunk himself. He turned around slowly in the silence. The men moved forward.

"All right, swabbies," he said thickly. "The rest of you clear the area before we call the wagon."

Behind him the two boys lay on the sidewalk. One of them had fallen forward from a kneeling position, like a penitent.

The men came on, and the marine placed his hand on his pistol holster, edging closer to his companion. The latter muttered angrily at the blond marine, but as the murmur increased he too placed one hand on his holster and with the other reached for his whistle. The men hesitated, and Stark, still coming, found himself at the forefront. He kept moving.

"Come here, you stupid bastard," Stark said to the first marine, his voice so choked as to be all but inaudible. He cleared his throat with a painful grating cough, as before him faces, howling in the inchoate roar, loomed and spun in the green and orange lights of his huge drunkenness. Joyfully he plunged forward, only vaguely aware, now that the rage was on him, of the two prostrate forms that had unleashed it. "You stupid goddam bastard," his voice said more loudly as the pistol appeared. "You stupid goddam belt-happy sonofabitch of a gyrene bastard—"

Gioncarlo and two other men reached Stark and held him as the second marine blew his whistle. The sailors shouted their derision, but a few started to move away. At the sound of an answering whistle down the street most of them retreated openly. The rest, self-conscious and shamefaced and still angry, milled around a minute longer, urging Stark and Gioncarlo to come with them. "C'mon, fellas," one of them said, "we ain't goin to do them boys no good by gettin our ass thrown in the brig." "Tonight of all nights," another said.

And then a voice said, "Come on, Charlie, why beat your brains out tryin to play the hero?"

Stark whirled about, in time to see Raditzer's face float up like a carnival mask between the shoulders of two larger men. Before Stark could speak, the pale face wheedled, "Come on, Charlie, come with me, come say hello to Myrna." And then, leaving Stark speechless, sobered, Raditzer disappeared, as if, after all, he had only been an apparition.

"Nobody's going to call me no stupid bastard," the blond marine was saying to Stark.

"You stupid bastard," Stark refuted him, for the sudden appearance of Raditzer had tempered his outrage, hardened it. It seemed to him that all the frustration and pointlessness of his war was focused in the one brutal, senseless act committed by this man. The marine glowered back at him. He had replaced the pistol, and now he was tossing his stick lightly in his hand. "I'm going to the guardhouse with these kids," Stark said. "I'm going to put this man on report, and I have a dozen witnesses."

"Not no more you don't, sailor," the second marine said sympathetically. He nodded at the disappearing men. "You only got your buddy here."

"I have you too," Stark said, shifting his gaze for the first time.

The man shrugged uncomfortably and turned to Gioncarlo. "Get lost, Mac," he said. "You're just askin for trouble hangin around here now." He glanced at Stark. "I know how you feel, all right, but they ain't nothin you can do."

"Why don't you and your apeman pal take them sticks of yours," Gioncarlo inquired, "and wrap them in barbed wire, and shove them—"

The blond marine stepped forward, hiking at his belt, but his companion barred him roughly, laying a nightstick across his chest. This second man was very big, with a broad neck and thick ears, and now he pointed the stick at Gioncarlo. "They ain't nobody goin to work your buddy over in the wagon, if that's what you're worryin about, sonny. So take off now. Beat it."

Gioncarlo stood there, obstinate, until the wagon appeared. The two boys were laid out on the benches. When Gioncarlo tried to follow Stark inside, the big marine seized him bodily and set him down on the street. He rapped the wagon wth his stick, and it started forward. The marine swung up on the tail-gate as Gioncarlo came for him. "So long, sailor." Grinning, he touched the tip of his nightstick to his forehead.

In the dark van the blond marine sat himself too close to Stark. "Try something," he said huskily.

"You drop that stick and holster belt and I will."

The other marine leaned toward them. "Shut up," he said. When the blond man glared he said to him, "Listen, you made enough of a mess as it is. You think I'm goin to lie to save your neck, you got another think comin."

One of the boys was trying to sit erect. The other was already sitting up. He looked sick and frightened.

"Well, let 'em go then," the blond man was complaining to his companion. "So maybe I acted sort of hasty. Let's let 'em go. I mean, the war's over, for Chrissake, they was only celebratin."

"Now he tells us," the big marine said disgustedly. He shrugged. "You want to drop it?" he said to Stark.

"No. He's going on report."

"How about them kids? You want to be hard-nosed about this thing, sailor, them kids are goin to spend the night in the brig, maybe lose their liberty pass altogether."

"What a headache I got," one of the boys said. "They didn't have to go and do that, we was only having a little fun."

"You heard them," the other said. "You want to go to the brig, or what? We only just begun a two-day pass."

"Yeah, I know, I know." The first boy turned to the big marine, silhouetted in the back of the van. Like his friend, he did not look at the other man at all. "You want to let us out now? I feel kind of sick."

Stark said, "You mean you guys want to pretend the whole thing never happened?"

But the big marine had already pounded on the cab, and the wagon jerked to a stop. The two boys got out, and Stark climbed slowly after them. "Find another cap," the big marine warned them.

"Pin a medal on your buddy," Stark said angrily. "He's a credit to the lousy Corps."

"We get all kinds," the marine said affably. "You got some foul balls in the Navy too, my friend." The wagon started slowly off down the strange street. "So don't get in such a uproar about life, you want my advice, sailor. Let the other guy sweat it out hisself. They ain't nobody lookin out for you." He waved, and Stark lifted his hand, smiling sourly.

One of the boys was coughing for attention. "Listen, chief, it ain't that we don't appreciate you standin up for us," he said. "It ain't that at all. But we don't want no more trouble, we just want to have a little fun. We been at sea since May," he added eagerly, "we seen combat and everything."

His friend was sitting on the curb, holding his head and moaning.

"How old are you guys?" Stark said.

"Just turned nineteen. Him too."

"Him too. Well, I'm twenty-six myself, and I never heard a shot fired in anger, what do you think of that?"

"I guess I'd say you was pretty lucky," the boy said pompously, wrinkling his brow.

"You guess you'd say I was pretty lucky."

"Gee, I don't know. I mean, I don't see what you're so sore at, it ain't you was hit. All I know is, my head hurts and I feel sick and I don't want no more trouble. I ain't even got a cap, and maybe we're goin to get run in again, how do I know?"

"Here," Stark said. He clapped his own cap hard on the boy's head.

"Well, thanks," the boy called as Stark started away. He made no attempt to refuse the cap or even to ask what Stark would do without one.

"Nothing's too good for our boys," Stark said. But the remark displeased him, and he let it trail off unheard.

Bareheaded, he felt a little better. Outside the law, even in this token way, he felt almost a renegade, and by the time he had made his way through the back alleys to the Adams car he was singing. He was on a two-day pass himself, and he did not permit himself to think too much as he drove toward Raditzer's, paying small attention to the speed limits and street signs. At one point he slowed to address two members of the shore patrol. "Look, men," he said, lifting both hands from the wheel to point at his head, "no cap."

"I heard you won the war singlehanded," one of them said good-naturedly. "Now go somewhere and sleep it off."

But the other said, "Where'd you get a car, sailor? Pull over."

"I'm an admiral," Stark said, "cunningly disguised as a ship's service laundryman, third class."

"C'mon, pull over. Hey!"

"Another time maybe," Stark called. He gunned the car as the whistle blew, glancing back as he turned the corner. One of the men was peering after the car, shading his eyes under the street light, and Stark thought for the first time about the license plate.

No good will come of this, my boy. No goddam good.

At Raditzer's he parked the car behind the kitchen and went into the bar. Soldiers, sailors, and marines were shouting on all sides, and he glimpsed Raditzer in his dark glasses, his arms draped on the shoulders of two customers and his mouth fixed in a smile. Raditzer caught Charlie's eye and glanced significantly at Myrna, who was singing her little heart out over the din. *Aloha oe.* She smiled at him, raising her eyebrows, and when she finished the last *aloha* came straight up to him. Her dress was so tight that it clung separately to each large, onrushing thigh.

Holy smoke, I'm done for.

"Hell-o, Char-lie."

"*Aloha* yourself. How's tricks, Myrn?"

"Why, I'm just fine, I'm sure."

"Well, you *look* fine. VAHINE NO TE VI." Woman with mango. It was true. She had the same thick smoky languor, the elliptical, dark eyes neat as smooth sea pebbles, the startled nostrils, the carved ridges between nose and wide high upper lip, the cool, full mouth, all of this tarnished badly and—in an effect like that of the black stockings on the green-skinned harlots of Toulouse-Lautrec—rendered perversely desirable by the cheaply bleached blond hair, the orange lipstick, the garish Western name.

"Myr-na," she insisted, savoring it, breathing it, in her innocence.

She was a mess, all right, as Gioncarlo had said, but a mess in which he meant to wallow, God help him, until he was blue in the face.

"It need the big victory party to bring you back, Char-lie, I guess."

"That's right. What time do you get off, Myrna?"

"Now, honey, Rad told me you already got a nice lady-girl stateside for—" She paused coyly, misinterpreting his grunt of displeasure. Wincing, unable to stop her, he watched her slap the back of one hand twice into the palm of the other. "For pom-pom," she concluded, sighing, and recommenced her aimless humming.

"*Who* told you?" he said at last.

"Rad."

"Rad, eh?"

"Mister Rad Raditzer, the boss. Your friend. *You* know. You mad with me, Char-lie?"

"Hell, no, I'm in love with you, Myrna. You and I are going somewhere to celebrate Hiroshima. We're going to celebrate the great victory of democracy and God over the yellow peril, if you know what I mean."

She snuggled next to him, hiking a hip onto his bar

stool. "Tell me where we goin, honey." She kissed his ear, and he shivered all over like a horse.

"Why, we're going to Punaluu, Myrna, where the sun is bright and the sea is clean and the surf is white and the *humu-humu-nuku-nuku-apawaa* goes swimming by, and we're going to subsist on *papios* and *papayas*."

Myrna was enchanted. "Like a honey-moon," she breathed.

He stopped smiling. "No," he said.

"Char-lie, you so funny."

Much later she accompanied him to the car. Behind them, in the bright doorway of the kitchen entrance, danced Raditzer's black silhouette.

"Charlie? Where you goin, Charlie?"

The voice was forlorn, incredulous, the voice of a child in the first apprehension that it is being left behind. It rose swiftly to a screech.

"How about Charlotte, Charlie? Christ!"

They roared up out of the lights and jangle of victorious Honolulu on the steep road through the mountain jungle to the Pali. The high wind struck them, and a cold moon flew. Stark did not hesitate at the pass but plunged down demoniacally around the turns toward the far lights at Kaneohe. In the valley he turned westward on the silent road, along still canefields and past black lagoons filling silently in the tide, across moon shadows of the jagged ridges, the outposts of the huge volcano of Oahu, which ages ago had risen from the deeps.

A feral dog, three-legged, fled the light.

The girl clung to his rigid arm. At the Pali her relentless humming had risen to a moan of apprehension, but she dared not interfere. To comfort her, he placed his arm about her neck and his hand upon her breast.

"It's just as I thought," he said admiringly and was startled by the cruel note in his own laugh. "Woman with mangoes."

"Char-lie?"

Then he felt sorry and hugged her sincerely. "I was saying that you were beyond my wildest dreams," he murmured and smiled gently.

She sighed and again began to hum. " 'Love-ly hula hands,' tum-te-tum-te-tum, TEE, tum, tum . . ."

The road across the palm grove to the beach cottage was wind-strewn with bowed fronds. They humped and cracked beneath the wheels. Stark wondered if Robert Ariyoshi was awake in his shack beyond the trees. He opened the car door to hand his true love out, but she had no idea what he was doing and barged past him. He realized now that she was drunk, as drunk as he was. She staggered across the grass on her high heels, staring up at the sharp palm patterns on the sky, spinning crazily and waving one leg to keep her balance, and hiccuping. Charlotte, long, long ago in Mexico, had walked on the night seashore like a child.

"You hear something?" Myrna demanded loudly, raising a finger to her lips.

"That's the North Pacific on the outer reef," he told her, "the night wind in the palms, the moon and earth."

"Oh," she said. "Don't it ever stop?"

"Never, never, never," he said fervently. "Now come inside, Myrna, before you catch cold in that alluring dress of finest oriental silks."

"Oh," she repeated. "I know what you after, Charlie-bad-boy." She lifted the back of one hand and poised it above the other.

"You're a deep one, all right, Myrn."

"Pom-pom!" she exclaimed triumphantly.

Charlotte and Charlie. Shar and Char.

But he knew it was too late. Looking at her, the musky opulence of her, he knew just how late it was.

How many times—there was so much of her, thick and white, like an Ingres harem, and he had to devour it all. His need itself excited her, for his love was random, headlong. Oo, honey, NOW. Together they struggled with his demon, raging back and forth across the *lanai*, which leaped in fits and starts to the center of the room. The last time, exorcised, he stroked her poor fevered head with his weak hand until she had subsided.

The light was gray when he hid himself in sleep, but moments later the world tapped implacably on the bamboo screen. He did not wish to wake ever again, but after a little while, coughing on the sour smell of sweat and jasmine, he forced his eyes open. A short white arm was crooked across his throat. Convulsively he rolled out from beneath it and sat up. His head lolled hideously, and the room turned black. She's strangled me to death, he thought, I'm giving up the ghost.

Tap, tap, tap.

He opened his eyes again, heart pounding. Surely it was Charlotte's father, outraged, with a horsewhip. No, it was Robert Ariyoshi. There he was—Stark could see him through the shutters—smiling expectantly at the bamboo screen. How fine that was, for a grown man to smile as innocently as that, unselfconsciously, out of pure anticipation. He remembered his own cheap remark the night before about the yellow peril, and groaned aloud.

"Yes," he said, his voice guttural with sleep and whisky.

"Mis' Stock? Ho, Mis' Stock? Bew-ful morning! You wan' go fishing Robert Ariyoshi for *papio?*"

"Oh, no, Robert, thanks. I just got to bed. Thanks anyway." He wondered how Robert could smile at all, with Hiroshima burning still, could wish to take the atom's henchman fishing for *papio*. But then,

Robert was an Oriental, and doubtless wise enough to hold no grudge against a laundry worker. Days later it occurred to Stark that way out there in remote Punaluu, without a telephone, Robert Ariyoshi had probably been still unaware of the holocaust in his homeland.

"Okay, Mis' Stock. Good-bye, Mis' Stock."

"Good-bye, Robert."

God be with you, Robert.

The fisherman turned, still smiling, his brown face creased with weather wrinkles, and walked away under the palm trees to the sparkling lagoon.

"Who was that?" Myrna muttered. "Where am I?"

"You're in romantic Punaluu, on your honeymoon," Stark said, pitching out of bed and making his way to the kitchen for water. "And that was Robert Ariyoshi, a friend of mine, who wanted to strew our sylvan bower with orchid leis."

"Char-lie, I feel so bad. My stomachs. My head." She made evil smacking sounds with her mouth. "Char-lie, you go crazy with me last night, you like a wild man, you know something?"

"He wanted to heap breadfruits at your pearly feet."

"I don't understand you, honey. I don't understand."

Honey and Heinie. Hein and Hon.

Then he stood over her, drinking the flat water, feeling mean. "Good morning, Myrna dear," he said as gently as he was able. His smile was dreadful to him.

The bed was a cornucopia, overflowing with unabashed stale flesh. She was loose and puffy, and he was tempted to think that she revolted him, all coming apart like this, but his own flesh was unrepentant, and he was forced to look away. Behind him, he heard her wrench the sheet to cover herself.

"You sorry, Char-lie?"

"Of course not. It was wonderful."

"I think Rad was right. You thinking about your nice lady-girl stateside. All you want me for is making pom-pom, you like all the joes." She had a fit of coughing. "And I thought you are so different, Charlie." She lay back, folding her arms across her tired breasts. "So different." To console herself, she hummed a sad slow song—*po-hai ke a-loha* . . .

He longed to forget her wild, inarticulate declaration of true love, called out to him in the night like a cry of pain, which he, expedient even in his drunkenness, had pretended not to understand, had rewarded with the affectionate grunts of lechery. Nor could he dismiss the last deadening irony, that his artless native girl had been a wretched lover. If, imagining herself in love, she had been shy, or if in his swinishness he had inhibited her, that was only part of it. Physically if not spiritually, his exotic flower of the isles had already resigned herself to the dim, flaccid sensualities of the ungifted whore.

"You think I are not nice or something?"

No, that's not it. No, Myrna, no, Myrna, no.

"Don't, Myrna." He lay back and kissed her shoulder, but he could not face her. "You're a very nice girl indeed."

She sighed. "Rad told me that very first night you come, be nice to Char-lie."

"Did Rad tell you to go to bed with Charlie?"

"No, he talked about your lady-girl. He joke me all the time. He say a man like his friend Charlie never touch a girl like me. And now you make me feel so bad."

"I'm sorry, Myrna. I don't mean to."

"I think I sleep a little, Charlie. I got to work to-night."

"All right, Myrna."

In the cold sun he lunged into the water and struck out toward the reefs. He had no strength, and the sea did not refresh him. Still he swam on, stabbing the water viciously with his arms, gritting his teeth, until he wondered if he would ever regain the shore. He swam farther, heavily, then thrashed wildly around, glaring back at the fierce mane of dawn light on the mountain spines. A cry of self-disgust burst from him, and he struck at the soft, resilient water.

Across the lagoon the fisherman stood up in his skiff and shouted. His silhouette was black against the red rays of the rising sun, imminent as an explosion behind the etched outline of the headland to the eastward, as if the fireball of the atom had carried around the world.

"*Kaku!*"

The word skipped like a flat stone across the water. *Kaku!* The Japanese extended his arms violently, then pointed at the water with his seaward hand and with the other hoisted by the gills a long gleaming silver fish. "*Kaku!*" He dropped the fish and waved Stark toward the shore with an agitated backhand motion of his arm.

"Go way!"

The cry rolled eerily across the water, echoing.

"Go way!"

Stark retreated toward the shore, sipping in his breaths in small, tight gasps. The lagoon was roiled by strong offshore winds and was the opaque smoky color of green sea glass. It seemed primordially hostile, like the black peaks and the raw red horizon. In this water the barracuda, unable to make him out, were unpredictable. He swam on, swallowing a surge of panic. Somewhere not far away slid a coasting, long-jawed shadow, and another, perhaps, hung suspended, indecisive, in the murk between his out-stretched fingers and the shore. His fingers cramped, and once his knees drew up spasmodically to protect his naked stomach. Exhausted, he let his legs drift down and treaded water. One foot touched a coral head, recoiled, and he struggled on, near frenzy, to the beach.

They drove back in the afternoon, forsaking the Pali for the shore road around the island and approaching the city by way of Koko Head and Waikiki. He left Myrna at her house in the back streets, where a group of Kanakee children clustered around to stare at them.

"Brothers and sisters," Myrna said. To them she murmured, "Say hello to Char-lie."

"Hello, Char-lie."

"Hello," Charlie said.

In flat, nasal voices, not unlike those of parrots, the children sang Charlie a dirty version of the "Washington Post March," acquired from the serv-icemen. Stricken, Myrna tried to stop them. "What you want Char-lie should think?" she pleaded. "What you want Char-lie should think?"

One little girl hoisted her shift above her waist

and gestured. "You make pom-pom with Big Vahine, Joe?"

Huge tears came to Myrna's eyes and would not fall. The children watched her in suspenseful silence. Then she ran clumsily through arid chickens and limp dooryard weeds toward the thin house, adjusting the dress with its bold slit upon her car-cramped hips. Charlie followed her at a distance, and fiercely she awaited him behind the rusty screen.

"Did I ask for money? Did I?"

"No."

"I never in all my life," she mourned. "I never did."

"I know," he said.

Stark stopped at the first bar and ordered a Tom Collins. He had several. Then he remembered the Adamses and returned the car. Carter Adams told him that the shore patrol had telephoned to ask if such-and-such a license plate was his, and, if so, was the car stolen? He had said no, it wasn't, but on request had given them Stark's name and Pearl Harbor base. Worried, he had taken the other car and gone over to Punaluu, where Robert Ariyoshi told him that Stark had been there. In the cottage, he said, he had put two and two together. Adams paused. Finally he suggested that his hospitality had been abused.

Stark nodded in agreement. He extended his hand, and Adams, startled, took it. Then Stark started off down the driveway. Adams called after him. He understood why Stark was celebrating—the war and all—and to come and see them before too long.

Half turning as he walked, Stark waved, and the turn dizzied him. He felt shaky and weak of soul. He went to Raditzer's, but, ashamed to face him—and this, he thought, was surely the most incredible of his ignominies—he did not have the stomach to go in. He went to a small bar down the street, where by nightfall he was drunk all over again. He drank alone. When he knew he could not take another without falling, he wandered out into the streets and started toward the edge of town.

The Japanese park, like an eye in the hurricane of celebration, was still and silent. Stark reeled down through its tropical night shadows and pitched across the corner of the footbridge into the trench.

"Shit," he said emphatically when he sat up, soaked to the waist. He fought a wild impulse to laugh violently or cry. The fall had frightened him, though he was unhurt, and now his heart stopped as he heard a calm voice from somewhere opposite, in the gloom beneath the bridge.

"That ain't the half of it, man," it said.

"Jesus, I'm surrounded!" Stark felt for the dark wall. The voice did not answer, and at last he said, as calmly as he could, "You been here long?"

"A long, long time, I guess," the voice said, infinitely embittered, like that of some sulking river demon. "I guess I been waitin on somebody like you to keep me company."

"Listen, I can't even see you, you must be in over your head." Stark peered dazedly into the shadows. "Everything's gone black or something."

"That's my natural-born color you lookin at, man. I come that way."

"No offense meant, pal."

"I didn't take none, Buster Brown."

On a fallen stone beneath the bridge the silhouette sat, hands on knees, upright and still as a wooden fetish. *Varua*. Uneasy, Stark stood and made his way a little closer.

PARUA NA TE VARUA INO.

"You just going to sit there all night, watching?"

"I'm just gone to sit tight so I don't fall over and get drownded. I'm a long, long way from home, man, and I been late a long, long time now." He sighed. "You got a dry smoke on you?" The light of the match illumined a white eye and a dark thin profile like carved mahogany. "Ain't no use in fightin life, man. I give up on that jazz long ago. You just got to let it carry you along." He blew the smoke in the direction of Stark's face. "They gone dirty they whites when they haul this nigger out, you know that, don't you?"

Stark had a cigarette himself, squatting back against the trench wall, silent. From where the dark man observed him, the other cigarette glowed in the darkness, and above their heads, from far away beyond the bridge, the horns and music, the lights and headlong voices, filtered through the restless leaves of night.

The figure spoke, in the toneless voice of an oracle. "Man, I been reading where the Big Bomb saved the world for all us God-fearin people."

Stark was silent.

"You think ol' God want us to win that bad?"

"No," Stark said, "I don't."

"Somebody got to pay," the voice said. "They is somebody got to pay."

In the water, with its mild algae odor, the moon's beam glittered like a knife. Stark felt strangely removed from the world and, like the man near him, in no hurry to return to it. They waited there like sentinels.

To the south the livid stars pulsed, three-dimensional, stars that until now had always wheeled below the horizons of his northern consciousness. One of the new constellations—it sprang forth from the sky—was the Southern Cross, and indeed the heavens were full of crosses. A second and third were luminous on each side of the first, although these were larger and less precise, vaguely askew. To the east of the short bar of the Southern Cross were two bright stars in a line, extending it. If the bar was perceived as an upright, and vice versa, a new cross could be seen. On this cross, perspectives were distorted, and the head of Jesus hung far forward, on his chest.

The voice said, "Man, they somebody high and mighty on this bridge lookin down on us poor intoxicated and ignorant trash. I c'n feel him."

It was true. A form had materialized above their heads, white as a seraph against the blue-black sky.

"Old Rad," Stark said at last and laughed quietly in despair.

"Christ, is that *you,* Charlie? It's me. It's Rad." He was terribly excited. "Listen, we got to get you out of there! Listen, it's lucky I was just on my way back—aw, Christ," he moaned, "I never thought I'd see *you* in there, not *you,* Charlie!"

"Here, give us a hand—" Stark jumped and caught the bridge edge with his fingertips. The wood cut him, and Raditzer's grip on his wrist was weak. "Grab my jersey," Stark said, hauling himself farther in exasperation, until his chin rested on the boards.

"Listen, I can't help you, Charlie, you're too big for me. What did you want to go and get yourself in a mess like this for anyway?" Raditzer suddenly let go, and after a moment Stark dropped back. The queer odor of the trench rose to his nostrils.

Above, arms folded across his chest, Raditzer shook his head. "I talked to Myrna, Charlie," he began.

"I hope you gave her my respectful greetings," Stark said, staring down at the water which came halfway to his knees. He longed to seize Raditzer's ankle and drag him down into the pit.

"I heard you gave her plenty besides greetings." The voice above him was insistent, unforgiving.

"Well, isn't that what you've been trying for three damned months to get me to do? You've been pimping right along."

Raditzer gasped audibly. "No, I ain't!" he exclaimed, and it was the disillusionment in his voice which twisted Stark's conscience. "Now don't go takin it out on me, Charlie!" He paused. "Christ, I thought you was different, I thought at least you and Charlotte—"

"What the hell do you know about Charlotte? Get the hell away from me!" Stark bellowed. "Go on, get the hell out of here, you dirty little bastard!"

Raditzer leaned over him, fists clenched. "You ain't in no position to call me dirty, Charlie, not after what you gone and done!" His voice broke, and Stark, peering up at the little man framed against the firmament, wondered if Raditzer could possibly be crying. Then Raditzer was gone, and the night was empty.

The figure behind Stark grunted speculatively, and Stark whirled on him.

"Just you relax now, man," the slow voice said, "just you relax. I don't know what your trouble is, but it sure as hell ain't with me."

Behind the town the mountains rose into the moonlit clouds, and above the clouds, a million years away, shone brilliant Sirius. Stark felt an aching premonition that he would never cross into those realms again. On the far side of the mountains lay Punaluu and a world he had longed for, a world which, once found, had no place in his reality. Unlike Gauguin, he had brought it nothing and had taken nothing away. Even the sketches he had made there he had destroyed, for they had been wispy and without life, without the strength he had to have—No—for a moment, as he stood stricken in the trench, his hope forsook him, and at the same instant a distant siren howled around some faceless corner and came nearer.

"That's The Man," the soft voice said. "He can take his time, 'cause Mister Black and Mister White ain't goin *no* place."

Stark leaned against the wall and waited.

In the brig he found some paper and wrote passionately to Charlotte—not, as he first assumed, because he had a bad conscience about Myrna, but because he was no longer in love with Charlotte, had perhaps never been in love with her. He had realized this with dread and dismay when Raditzer, on the bridge, had cried. And it was Raditzer, in his insane, vicarious adoration of a girl he had never seen, who had unwittingly pointed out the frailty, the expedience of Stark's own feeling for her. She had been so damned suitable, after all, lovely bright innocent Charlotte, in that lovely bright innocent world of his upbringing, in which, as his first experience away from it had taught him, he could never rest at peace again.

But if he was not in love with Charlotte, he loved her all the same, and he meant never to let her see the difference. In an attempt to recapture what he had lost, he described to her with longing the windward coast and especially Kailua, where he had always meant to go and now would not. It sounded so much like what it was, a distant beach visible from the mountains, veiled in salt mist from the sea. The blue-emerald water there would be streaked with black coral shadows, with a white ring of surf along the outer reefs, and a flight of golden plover would alight on it each fall, at the end of a long journey from Alaska.

For evading arrest in the Adams car, and for being disorderly and out of uniform, Stark was court-martialed, but because he had been celebrating patriotically the victorious conclusion of the war, his understandable exuberance was dealt with lightly. He was confined to the base for two months, on assignment to Raditzer's mess hall, where he was ordered to administer to the great vats and ovens a long-needed scouring.

Raditzer, as martyr, was at pains to forgive Stark his abuse, and Stark himself, apathetic, permitted their former relationship to resume. But Raditzer was now patronizing Stark, who not only had proved himself so mortal but had become the lowest and greasiest of untouchables in the hierarchy of the mess hall. The discrepancy in their positions seemed to inspire Raditzer to boast even more copiously than before about his restaurant in Honolulu. Apparently he felt that he cut a dashing figure on the base and that at last the world must recognize it. In fact, he was so indiscreet that Stark wondered whether a need for notoriety or a reckless masochism had possessed him. He warned Raditzer, too late, that the restaurant was certain to crash about his ears at any moment.

Within a matter of weeks an investigation was begun. Raditzer had covered his tracks well enough so that the Navy could not muster a court-martial, but he was nonetheless banished to Johnston Island, a remote coral atoll some seven hundred miles westward. Before he left he sought out Stark, as Stark, for some reason, knew he would.

Charlie had been shaving in the washroom when, feeling something behind him, he glanced up from the sink into the mirror. There stood Raditzer, so close that in that instant his own head and Raditzer's seemed attached to the same body.

He lifted the razor in a defensive spasm, and Raditzer moved back a little.

"They're sendin me out there to die, Charlie, and they ain't got nothin on me! I been framed! It ain't even constitutional!" Raditzer's small mouth was alive with anguish, and Stark noted with compassion, once again, the ragged teeth, the pale, dark-pored skin, the red nares of a nose much picked and —because of a sleepless phlegm—much blown, which made Raditzer somehow poverty-stricken even in demeanor. The eyes, however, were typically alert and hard. "Christ, guys have gone nuts on that lousy rock, you know that, and I'm the kind can't get along without my crowd, just like I told 'em. I won't last a week out there, and they know it. But you think they listened to me?" He shook his head, moaning bitterly. "Aw, no, not *them!*"

Stark stood patiently, gazing at the mirror, as Raditzer's voice rose to almost a scream. "They always crucify the little guys, ain't that a fact? A guy that come into life with nothin, never had a chance he didn't make for hisself, and what do they do? They send this guy of all guys to Johnston, just so's he can't better hisself none—" He paused, and his hand strained toward Stark but did not touch him. "Christ, Charlie, look at me when I talk to you, don't go turnin your back on a fella like the way they done, just because you got dough and education and advantages. I mean, ain't I human, just like you, for Chrissakes?" He seized his hair as if on the point of lifting his own body off the floor for Stark's inspection. "Well, ain't I, Charlie? Ain't I born free and equal too?"

He clawed at Stark's shoulder, but drew back immediately when Stark stiffened. "I mean, you're the only guy understands me, Charlie, and you think you're too good for me just because I ain't never had what you had in life—"

Gioncarlo, down the way, rapped his razor loudly on the sink. He belched elaborately, and a few others snickered.

"You're out of your mind," Stark said. "It's not that. I just don't see how I can help you."

"You could have gone in there with me when they called me in. We could have made up some lie or other, ain't that right, if you was a real buddy to me? But not you, you don't even want to talk to me in front of these guys, you don't want to admit about us bein buddies!" His voice rose again, while his eyes appraised the silent, attentive faces in the washroom. The hostility in the air, Stark realized, was not for Raditzer alone. "You think you're Godamighty because you was born with a silver spoon in your mouth, but you ain't even got the milk of human kindness!" He paused for a moment, as if gauging the effect of this outburst on the other men, then regarded Stark briefly. Well, how did you like *that?* his expression, triumphant, seemed to say. And he scurried away, leaving Stark, who had never once turned around, to stare stupidly at his own soap-smeared visage in the glass.

I know you, Charlie.

Afterward he remembered little of what those last months had meant, retaining only the damp sounds and steamy odors that formed the background of Stark's War. Even when his liberty was restored he sought out neither Myrna nor the Adamses. He gave up painting—for the time being, he answered himself, without much confidence. He did not visit Punaluu again and passed most of his liberties shouting drunkenly in the byways of Waikiki.

Once, long after Punaluu, he chartered a fishing boat with Gioncarlo and Steve R. Kubichek and crossed the rough Kaiwi Channel to Molokai. The boat's captain pursued the frigate birds, which traced in turn the schools of flying fish, pursued from below by other silent hunters. When a dark bird hung above the wake, it was usually a matter of moments before the sea astern would gleam with emerald fire, and the *mahi-mahi* itself, the dorado or dolphin, would crack a white furrow in the dancing chop, flashing toward the bait. The resplendent fish, boated, would gasp away its color with its life, fading from emerald to sapphire, then swift as a rainbow to gold, yellow, silver, and at last a dirty gray. The dorados struck hard off the Molokai coast, to the west of the leper settlement on its bleak peninsula beneath iron cliffs. The whitecaps were sun-struck that afternoon, and falls of fresh water fumed down the dark rock into the sea, but the leper huts in their limbo between sea and sky depressed the men, and so did the gray dorados. "When my fish come in, he looked just great," Kubichek remarked, "but now he looks just like Raditzer." Because he felt seasick Kubichek said this with a kind of grim, game despair, and the others laughed. But afterward Stark was silent and thought longingly of Punaluu. At Punaluu he would not have seen the bait fish or *mahi-mahi*, only the long gaunt birds, but the swift fish would be there below, flying and flashing through their realms in the pure morning ocean. Life had carried him on so swiftly, and now Punaluu was lost to him forever, like remote places one glimpses on a journey and, staring backward through small windows, realizes one will never see again.

In 1946, less than a year after the war had ended, both Stark and Gioncarlo were ordered back to the United States for discharge, and, as it happened, their ship was once again the *General Pendleton*. Standing with their gear in the bright summer sun of the Navy Yard, they regarded her with admiration, riding trimly in a fresh coat of gray paint against the sad background of isolated masts and rusting hulls which, in that year, still marked the oily grave of the Pearl Harbor dead.

Gioncarlo's face was harder, taking shape, and it

seemed to Stark that he looked very much now as he always would until the day he died. "I only hope they cleaned up after me since the last time," he remarked, and they both laughed.

"I wonder if Raditzer will be on her this time too," Stark said a little later. "I mean, he's got the same number of points as we do, he's due to be shipped home." Daydreaming, he had manufactured something to say out of politeness to Gioncarlo, and it was only later, when Raditzer actually appeared, that he wondered how close this possibility had been to the surface of his mind. He remembered thinking of other things—the strong sense of pleasure he derived from industrial waterways and piers, the smell of old hawsers and of creosote on the pilings, the oil on the black harbor surface, the winches and great drums of cable, the sounds and colors that accompanied embarkation. He had thought also, all over again, of the difference between his war and the war represented by the desolation still visible around him, a war that men very similar to himself and Gioncarlo had not survived. Perhaps there had even been a Raditzer in that war, whining ignobly to the last. And behind all these thoughts lay the prospect of Charlotte, hanging back behind more immediate impressions only to drift forward in each lull, like some delicate smell of flowers on a windy summer's day, bringing excitement and a pleasurable sensation in the chest and throat which made him want to cry out his hope for them aloud.

"Raditzer?" Gioncarlo looked incredulous.

Stark shrugged, lost in thoughts of Charlotte. He cherished her now, was touched by so many remembered actions, postures, the way she crouched on elbows and knees to read the Sunday papers, or the way, when she was cross, she would poke her head out at him around doorways and corners to fix him with that absurd angry glare, until both of them, at the same instant, would turn away in order not to laugh and then laugh anyway. Yes, yes, everything was going to be all right. Still, it worried him that Charlotte, ever intuitive, had seemed to divine the metamorphosis their marriage had undergone—though she said nothing—and had not really been consoled by the barrage of love with which, more and more sincerely, he had tried to make amends. The battle, pitched in silence, was apparently not over, for her letters left with him an effect of uneasy suspense, as if they had all ceased abruptly in mid-sentence and been left unsigned.

"Raditzer! I'll tell you about that guy," Gioncarlo said. "He—oh, God, Charlie, I just don't see why you bleed over him is all," Gioncarlo exclaimed suddenly, noticing Stark's expression. "You guys are as different as night and day."

Stark glowered. "Why don't a couple of you beat him up then, if that will make you feel better? Maybe knee him and gouge him a bit while you're at it?"

"Somebody must have by this time." Gioncarlo, shrugging off Stark's sarcasm, peered upward as a whistle blew aboard the *Pendleton*. Some shouted orders down from the foredeck as the men nearest the gangplank shouldered their duffels. "Maybe they killed the creepy bastard, out on Johnston."

But Raditzer, Stark knew, had survived Johnston Island. Unsavory accounts of him—his name was a near-legend—had drifted back with the men passing through Pearl Harbor. When Stark first heard the familiar voice, he was lying in his berth in the troop holds, storing away in his mind the last view of Hawaii, seen at sunset. The channel between islands had been crossed, and the leper colony beneath the cliffs of Molokai lay on the starboard beam as the ship dropped off the bright sea path of the sun into the twilight. The island of Maui fell away, a purple shadow to the southward, and the last sharp-winged silhouette of a great frigate bird traversed the silent wake. Stark had paused briefly at the hatch, contemplating a foredeck no longer encumbered by the landing craft of war but sweeping cleanly to a bow pointed across calm seas toward home. He took a deep breath in vague regret, nostalgia, for the Islands, for a time and place that had never been quite real. Then he had gone below.

And Raditzer had come, preceded by that voice,

that wail of laughter, that ignorance, feigned or otherwise, of his own exile. Turning slightly in his bunk, Stark watched Raditzer's progress down the aisles, the loud greetings met with surprised silence by men who did not know him, with sullen silence by the men who did.

"Anybody seen an old buddy of mine, a guy name of Charlie Stark?"

This time, though still some distance away, Raditzer raised his eyes as if he had known the location of Stark's bunk from the beginning. For a strange second they exchanged a look devoid of greeting. But in this look Raditzer established once more the bond between them and dared Stark to repudiate him. Then he dropped his eyes momentarily, raised them again, and with a new expression cried out, "By Christ, I found him! There's the old bastard now!" And he loosed a hoarse salvo of foul appellations which, in the usage of war and in any other mouth, might have been deemed affectionate, but which Stark recognized in a sickening insight as meant sincerely in a quite different way. Then Raditzer was upon him, his hand gripping Stark's knee and his raw smile working. His eyes, wet and high colored, passed coldly over Stark. "Jesus," he kept saying, "Jee-sus," shaking his head in simple-minded wonderment and pleasure.

Stark swung his legs out of his bunk, shaking off Raditzer's hand and swinging his shoes idly at the level of Raditzer's mouth. Perched high above the passageway, he felt foolish, aware that every man in sight was eying him, demanding silently what the strange affinity with Raditzer might be. Yet he would see it out.

"You're looking great, Charlie-boy, never better," Raditzer was saying, his eyes now fastened on the shoes swinging before his face, as if he meant to lick them. Raditzer's whites were still tailor-made, his cap was cocked jauntily upon one eye, and he was affecting sideburns. All the other men wore denims. Raditzer glanced about him with contempt. "Pretty soft war all you fellas had," he muttered for Stark's benefit.

Stark cleared his throat. "They still fighting on Johnston Island, are they?"

"Well, I was closer to the war than you guys, you know that, don't you? I wasn't layin around with no Myrna on no goddam Waikiki."

"Raditzer, the war was over before you ever left Pearl Harbor."

Raditzer tapped Charlie's shoe, lowering his voice to a whisper. "Listen, Charlie, I ain't sayin I seen action exactly, only a lot of these fellas think I did, and I'm kinda stringin 'em along on it, know what I mean?" He raised his eyes to Stark's. "For a joke, kind of," he murmured. "For a joke. I got all these souvenir Jap weapons, see, and the fellas think I'm pretty salty. Only the joke's on them, get it?"

"And an excellent jest it is."

"Sure. The fellas never took me serious, like, and now they do. Get it?"

"I think so," Stark said, infinitely depressed.

"Sure. Hell, I knew I could count on you, Charlie, you old——." And raising his voice again, and coming as close as he ever did to looking Stark straight in the eye, Raditzer once again assaulted him with the foul endearments of manly affection, topping off the tirade with a bray of improbable merriment and an admiring shake of the head intended to convey to the men around them that Raditzer's pal, old Stark here, was certainly the comic spirit of the world, even though Stark himself, in full view of the assemblage, had quite clearly said nothing at all. Then Raditzer moved off, calling shrilly to Stark over his shoulder his hopes for a later rendezvous, picking his way fastidiously over stolid, hostile shoes like a cat negotiating a wet alley.

Across the way lay Gioncarlo, hands behind his head. He was glaring at Stark, and Stark, after a few moments, lay down again upon his back.

"I don't get it," Gioncarlo said. "I still don't get it. What in hell has that guy got on a guy like you?"

"With Raditzer," Stark said, almost to himself,

"you have only two choices, because you aren't going to change him. One choice is to tolerate him, on the grounds that he shares the human condition—"

"And the other is," Gioncarlo interrupted, "you kill him, on the grounds that he don't."

"I suppose so. You feel like killing him, Jack?"

"Yeah, I do, as a matter of fact. Every man on this ship does, from what I hear, and especially the guys who *really* seen action. Raditzer ain't foolin them for a minute, and they had about enough. I talked to some guys was on Johnston with him too, Charlie, and they all got pretty stories. So everybody's got it in for him, all except you, that is, Charlie you old———." He mimicked Raditzer's epithets in the tone in which, as he was shrewd enough to see, Raditzer had actually intended them. Stark sat up on his elbows. The two men watched each other.

"Maybe the rest of us ain't saints," Gioncarlo said, a shadow of real bitterness on his face. "Maybe we don't know enough about no-bless oblige. All I know is, you was once the best man in this outfit, all the guys thought so, and then you let this Raditzer suck around. And now it's gotten so that, bein *your* friend, even *I* ain't trusted."

"If that's what you're worried about—"

"I'm just sayin, don't be so goddam stubborn!" Gioncarlo roared, sitting up again. "And don't get *me* sore, because you're runnin out of friends. No-body asked you to pretend that guy was human, Charlie, let alone your buddy."

"No, I guess nobody did," Stark answered, feeling nonetheless that Raditzer *had* asked him, would al-ways ask him, and that Raditzer's plight was too grievous to be ignored.

And he knew that, despite Jack's violence, this reaction was shared in part by all the others—for the moment, Raditzer was still awarded the sort of tolerance ordinarily reserved for the sick and crip-pled. He had left behind him a wake of silence, a sort of brooding, angry bewilderment, but no man here, not even the brash Gioncarlo, had raised his voice against him, in a situation where a lesser fraud, braggart, and cheat would have been met by an avalanche of abuse. Some of the men followed Ra-ditzer with their eyes, and some regarded Stark. A few were battle veterans, stragglers from the hospitals and brigs of the Far East, and their silence was the most ominous of all.

There was a rumor about four of these men, that they had been involved in an officer's death, at Sai-pan. The officer had been seized at night and thrown into the sea. And it was true that the four kept to themselves, inseparable, though they appeared less fond of one another than enchained. Together, they had watched Raditzer, like a jury. One of them had a bayonet which he polished aimlessly by the hour with an oily rag, staring down at the metal floor between his feet.

This man's name was Carl, and according to Gion-carlo, who had struck up an acquaintance with Carl and his silent companions, he was not in his right mind. To deal with some secret and nameless enemy —imaginary, the others said—he had bought the bayonet from a marine. While Raditzer had been standing near his bunk, Stark noticed, Carl's hand was rigid on the bayonet blade, and his curious flat blue eyes had been focused on Raditzer, unblinking. Carl's friends—he seemed to be their leader, though he rarely spoke—had noticed this too, and had edged in closer.

But after all, Stark asked himself, what has Raditzer really done to any of us? He has done nothing.

He fell gradually into uneasy sleep, the muscles of his legs and arms bracing him rhythmically against the slow roll of the ship. The night sea above his head was calm, with only the long swells of remote storms rolling down across the bow from the northern oceans, to subside at last in the oblivion of green southern seas. The *Pendleton* rode onward through a great black sphere of phosphorus and stars, her bowlight rising and falling on the sky like a comet of good omen, while within the mass of her dark hull, beneath the ever-burning light, the cargo of men was carried toward the continent of home.

At midnight only Raditzer was still abroad, flitting down the passages in quest of communion with a man, any man, whom he might take unaware. Stark, wakeful, watched him, but closed his eyes tight whenever Raditzer passed him on his rounds. Other men, he sensed, watched Raditzer too.

A cry rose from the poker game in the empty compartment adjoining. Stark came fully to his senses and knew that he would sleep no more that night. Raditzer's restlessness had infected him, and there came with it a tremor of foreboding. He felt like gambling, indulging some angry notion of hurling away his money. To hell with it, he told himself dully, not quite certain what he meant. He climbed slowly from his bunk and dressed.

Approaching the archway to the next compartment, observing the silent men beneath a yellow lantern, he had a strong sense of a religious tableau, a triptych, which would come to life only when he stepped through the picture frame of the arch. He faltered, as if to enter was to set in motion some inalterable action. Then he stepped over the sill, and the men turned and acknowledged him at this moment. They were guarded, and their reserve was a rebuke, he knew, for his relationship with Raditzer. Gioncarlo was there, and did not greet him. The men, besides Gioncarlo, included Steve R. Kubichek and the four combat veterans transferred home from the Far East. The quiet man, Carl, even as he dealt Stark into the game, held his bayonet in its oily rag across his lap.

They had played quietly a little while when Stark became aware of Raditzer behind him. Like a moth attracted by the lantern, he stood agitating at the light's edge. The players refused to notice him, though Stark glanced up at him and nodded. It was only after Kubichek, sleepy, had stumped off to his bunk that Raditzer was allowed to make the seventh player. He sat himself, smiling joyfully, next to Stark. The stakes were large and growing larger, with no limit on the betting, and several of the men were getting drunk.

Raditzer increased the tension of the game immediately by flaunting a suspicious roll of bills and raising the bets so sharply that his winning, at first, appeared to be based on driving the other men out of the play. He was a poor winner, giggling and teasing, and he kept shifting position in a nervous way, thrashing about so ceaselessly that the man with the bayonet, wordless, at last pointed the weapon at his chest in an unmistakable order to sit still.

Nevertheless, in the endless ways peculiar to him, Raditzer continued to make himself objectionable. He refused to share the whisky smuggled aboard from Honolulu by its owner, a huge man they called Big Okie, who, irritated in the first place that he felt obliged to offer some to Raditzer, was enraged when Raditzer refused it, patronizingly, with an air suggesting that professional gamblers like himself never drank at the gaming table. Furthermore, Raditzer kept up an obscene, distracting chatter until warned a second time by the bayonet, at which point he began to hum instead what he considered suitable accompaniments to the mood of the man studying his hand. He kept his cap cocked over his eye in an affectation of jauntiness which annoyed Gioncarlo particularly, and once, when called upon to show his cards, tossed them airily into the lap of the heaviest loser, a balding man named Hoak whose fat looked hard.

Hoak looked down at the cards in his lap, then up at Raditzer, then down at the cards again. He sighed raggedly, controlling himself. "That was a mistake," he said.

But Raditzer, possessed, paid no attention to him. He pressed close to Stark, clutching his elbow, whispering a babel of poker jargon into his ear and snickering nonsensically, and pointing at the other men in illustration of his contempt, as if he and Stark were

in league against the rest. The players watched them
—Jimmy, who was dealing, thin and uncertain, with
a tic at the corner of his mouth, and Okie, licking his
lips stupidly, and Carl, the man with the bayonet, and
the stolid Hoak, and Gioncarlo, who glared at Stark
beseechingly. No one said a word. Stark sat quite
still, expressionless. Unwilling to repudiate Raditzer
simply to mollify the others, he neither listened to
him nor shouldered him away. It was only when Raditzer, after Stark had dropped out on a hand of
draw, displayed his own cards to Stark in a crude attempt at bluffing the other players that Stark struck
him sharply with his elbow.

"For Christ's sake, Raditzer," he murmured. "Play
your own game. Leave me out of it."

But Raditzer bobbed up and down delightedly, as
if Stark had instead confirmed his own high opinion
of his hand. He winked elaborately at Stark, implicat-
ing him further, when Okie folded on Raditzer's final
raise, then named his openers offhandedly and tossed
the cards face down to the next dealer. This time,
however, .as he reached for the pot, the flat of the
bayonet came down hard upon his wrist.

"Let's see them kings." Carl spoke for the first
time. "Your word ain't nearly good enough for me."

"What do you want to go and hurt a fella for,"
Raditzer whined, holding the wrist out like a broken
wing. "I told you, pair of kings."

"I know you did," Carl said. With the tip of the bayonet he flipped over Raditzer's hand, card by card. There were a deuce and a five of diamonds, an eight and king of clubs, and a jack of hearts.

The men stood up. Raditzer squeaked something about mistaking the jack for a second king but relapsed immediately into a frightened moan, as if aware that even if he were telling the truth he would not be believed. Stark could not imagine that Raditzer would have cheated so witlessly unless he had wanted to be caught. In any case, Raditzer's curious immunity was over. This he seemed to know himself, for he backed up against the bulkhead, speechless.

For a few seconds nobody said a word. Slowly the men formed a half-circle around Raditzer. Then Gioncarlo, the youngest and drunkest, and a heavy loser, lost his temper.

"I should have warned you guys," he shouted. "This Raditzer is a thief, and he ain't seen no combat neither. He's the dirtiest scum that ever crawled the earth, that's what he is, he don't deserve to live!"

The other players turned their gaze from Raditzer to Carl. Stark did the same, and found himself confronted by a madman. Carl's blue eyes, beneath faint eyebrows raised and drawn back tight, had gone dead flat, unblinking, and his breathing in the silence was quick and short, like panting. He took up the oily rag and ran it mechanically up and down the bayonet blade.

"Why, he ain't goin to," he answered Gioncarlo.

When Carl took a short step forward, shifting position, Raditzer uttered a little shriek, then cried out, "Charlie! Don't run out on me, Charlie!"

"Charlie," Hoak said reflectively. "Maybe Charlie was in on it too, huh, Charlie? It's easier for two guys to cheat than one, ain't that right, Charlie?"

"Maybe you'd like to try saying that again," Stark said, the incipient rage in him making his heart pound. He felt like fighting now in the same intense, fatalistic way that he had felt like gambling an hour before.

"Maybe I would, Charlie," Hoak said. "I'll let you know in a minute."

"That's right, Stark here's his buddy," Okie was saying. "He was sitting right alongside of him. Maybe he'd better go over there and stand alongside of him too."

"He ain't no buddy to Raditzer," Gioncarlo said, suddenly sober. "This guy's okay." To Stark himself he gave a furious, exasperated glance as if to say, You see, you see?

"Well, that's good," Okie said. "Because this boy Raditzer is goin over the side, and anybody stands in the way or don't want to keep his mouth shut is goin after him, ain't that right, Carl?" When Carl nodded,

Okie looked contemptuously at Stark. "You shore-station boys wouldn't know nothin about things like that, I guess."

Stark said nothing. He felt the sweat start out on his palms, like blood, and was afraid.

Big Okie smiled at him, and the smile hardened suddenly, fixed like a scar on the rough, red face. "You look like you don't believe me," he said. "Well, we seen it once ourselves, off Saipan." He turned to Carl. "Remember Saipan, Carl? The deep six. And nobody never said a word."

"Not until now," Carl said, and the big smile faltered.

None of the other players spoke. Hoak, the balding man, stared straight at the floor, arms folded on his chest. The thin man, Jimmy, stared upward, his fingernail scratching nervously on the denim of his inner thigh. Sensing Stark's gaze, he glanced away, clearly frightened, then glanced back again immediately, imploring, as if to say, For God's sake, save us all. Stark, struggling to think quickly, guessed that this man was more afraid of Carl than of his conscience and would be useless. He turned to Gioncarlo. The boy was watching him, frightened too, but his fear was obviously for Raditzer, and he seemed on the point of some desperate and fatal maneuver. Stark, lifting one hand slightly, cautioned him.

Now Okie, hoarse and foul-mouthed, was reviling

Raditzer, apparently trying to provoke a reaction, any reaction, which the men might seize upon to re-fire their rage. And Raditzer, cowering back, his mouth drawn tight in a round, black hole, glared wildly from Carl to Stark and began to whimper.

"Charlie," the voice came, "Oh, Jesus, Charlie!"

Still Stark said nothing. From the very beginning, less than a minute before, Stark's instinct had told him that he should not speak prematurely, that an ill-timed remark from a man considered friendly to Raditzer might prove fatal. Even worse, he realized, in the desperate lucidity that had replaced his shock, would be Raditzer's own exacerbating voice, and Raditzer was again on the point of speaking. Though Carl was observing him, he heard his own voice snap at Raditzer, "Be quiet." Okie said something in Carl's ear, his red face fierce, but Okie, Stark sensed, was preoccupied with working up his private courage for the killing. Only Carl, the small, fairhaired man with the bayonet, was resolved and calm, and perhaps the fat man, Hoak.

The latter cleared his throat. "We goin to do it, let's get on with it," he said, as if he would be neither happy nor unhappy either way.

Raditzer opened his mouth again, sinking weakly upon his knees, and staring at Stark alone, as if in this lay his salvation. Even in this moment of peril his eyes were hard, alert, even vindictive. But Stark turned to face Carl, who was daring him softly to identify further with Raditzer.

"Anything else you want to say, sailor, before he goes over the side? Because we'd like to know where you stand." Carl glanced at the other players, one by one, all but Gioncarlo, and when he heard no objection returned his gaze to Stark.

"You know where I stand already." Stark, too, glanced at the other men, one by one, and took heart from their expressions. Gioncarlo, biting his lip, came and stood pointedly at Stark's side. Nevertheless Stark's voice broke as he said to Carl, "I'm against it." He gasped for breath.

"What are you going to do about it, sailor?"

"I don't know yet."

"Maybe you feel like a long swim, sailor."

"You're not tossing Stark if I can help it, Carl," Gioncarlo blurted. "So you only got four against two."

"Three against three," the fat man said abruptly. "I ain't goin along with you on this Stark guy, Carl." He jerked his thumb at Raditzer. "This bastard, yes, if that's what everybody wants."

"It ain't the same like it was off Saipan, Carl," the thin man, Jimmy, said, still scratching himself, but shifting his hand, as the men faced him, to the region of his shoulderblades. "We ain't all shipmates here, we don't hardly know some of these guys"—he gestured apologetically toward the men now filling the arch of the compartment—"much less know we can trust 'em to be quiet."

"War's bad enough," Carl said intensely, "without gettin screwed by the guys on your own side."

"This ain't war now, Carl," Hoak reminded him gently. "The war's over. We're goin home."

Carl gazed coldly at Big Okie, who had been silent. Okie, as if lashed, said suddenly to the others, "You guys with us or ain't you? Because Carl and me can take care of this alone."

There was a stir, and Raditzer, who had kept his peace only by dint of clamping his teeth tight together, became hysterical. "They don't want to do it, them others, Carl, they don't want to murder a fella American that only made a mistake, they ain't no psycho case like you, Carl, they're just a bunch of lousy, frightened sonsabitches like me and Charlie Stark there, just ordinary fellas. They ain't no goddam lunatic like you, Carl—!"

Carl's friends stiffened, closing in on Raditzer. Carl, standing apart, said nothing. Big Okie laid a hand upon Carl's shoulder. "That settled it," he said, "that settled it."

Raditzer awaited them, spewing out his bitter oaths with a kind of suicidal ferocity, as if he meant to tell mankind his low opinion of it before departing for a better world.

Quickly and quietly among themselves, Carl's friends worked out the details of the execution, gauging as they spoke the faces of the men now filling the compartment behind Stark and Gioncarlo. Some of these men were combat veterans like themselves, and their faces were set, impassive. It don't matter what you decide to do, or whether I like it or not, each face seemed to say, because it ain't none of my business and I ain't seen nothin. Only one man, startled suddenly by what was about to happen, paled and withdrew. The rest gazed morbidly at Raditzer.

Stark took Gioncarlo's arm. "I'm going to belt him, Jack," he muttered, "and then push him at you. You do the same, and turn him over to Hoak, do you understand, Hoak. Make it look good."

Gioncarlo stared.

"Just do as I say," Stark snapped. He stepped forward and collared Raditzer, hauling him up onto his feet. "You miserable bastard," he said loudly, "you tried to make it look like I was in on it with you, didn't you—tried to pretend that we were friends. Well, we're not—"

In the instant before his fist struck Raditzer's face Stark wondered if his rage sounded as false to the other men as it did to himself, in that voice which he could not recognize as his own. Raditzer was so astounded that he raised no hand to defend himself, and his wide eyes simply stared at the coming blow.

Because Stark held him up he did not fall. Arms limp at his sides, he blinked as the blood sprang from his nose, then spat furiously into Stark's face.

Apparently Gioncarlo understood, for at this instant he shouted out, "I want a crack at him too, the lousy thief!" He spun Raditzer away from Stark and delivered a right cross to the side of the head. Raditzer reeled back against the bulkhead, coughing. He was trying to say something but could only emit a squeal. When he stumbled, almost falling, Gioncarlo seized him and hurled him at the broad chest of the surprised Hoak.

Hoak had at first called out contemptuously to Stark, suggesting that Stark had made a cowardly attempt to enlist himself on the safe side at the last minute. Now he looked uncertain. Bearlike, he held Raditzer to his chest as if the small man were a child. He seemed to guess what Stark had chanced, that if the men eased their outrage by striking Raditzer the will to kill him would be dissipated, and he seemed to know that it was up to him whether or not the maneuver would succeed. For a long moment he looked carefully at Stark and Gioncarlo. Then he made his decision with a slight shrug of his shoulders. Methodically, without heat, he doubled Raditzer with a short, swift punch to the stomach, then shoved him with his free hand at the thin man. "Hit him," he said. Jimmy struck Raditzer with a wild right hand, and this time Raditzer fell.

Big Okie, confused, glanced at Carl, then stepped forward, smiling a little, and grabbed up Raditzer's limp body by the shirt front. Raditzer's eyes, rolling open momentarily, sought out Stark's own, but were already too glazed to convey emotion of any kind. The big man propped him on his feet. He stepped quickly back, then forward again, all his weight behind his fist. There was a terrible, flat, meaty sound, and Raditzer, weightless, struck the bulkhead, spinning in a loose sprawl, face down, on the metal floor.

Okie, excited, grinned pleasurably at Carl. "You want a shot at him?" he said.

Carl did not answer. Since Raditzer's outburst he had neither spoken nor stirred. Now he turned his back on Okie, who stopped smiling, turned his back on them all, and walked slowly out of the compartment, in a dream. As he passed Stark he reached out lightly and put his hand upon Stark's arm, but he did not look at him and he said nothing.

In the silence everyone stared at Raditzer, who lay crumpled in the shadows beyond the lantern's yellow arc.

"I still say he's gettin off too easy." Big Okie spoke truculently though without much heart. "After what he said about old Carl and all. We got to protect Carl's interests."

"That's exactly what we done," Hoak said, looking up at Okie with cold, contemplative dislike. "His and ours both." He was crouched over the forgotten game, dividing Raditzer's winnings into six piles. The men watched him. When he was finished he nodded his head in Raditzer's direction, then looked at the thin man. "Go get his duffel, Jimmy, all his gear." When the man came back, Hoak took the souvenir weapons from him and tossed them on his palm, then dropped them loudly to the metal floor. He emptied the contents of the duffel and a cheap cardboard suitcase upon the weapons. Among the soiled denims and whites there were a full officer's uniform complete with battle ribbons, two pairs of Navy binoculars, a ship's chronometer, four watches, some pornographic magazines, a pair of lace panties, and, adhered to the bottom of the suitcase, a small, black-haired human scalp.

"He must have fallen in with some marines," Hoak said. Squatting over the pile, arms loose across his knees, he whistled. "I don't know about you guys," he said, "but an outfit like this don't make me feel it's very good to be alive." He was terribly angry, and his contempt was for himself, for all of Raditzer's fellow men, as well. He spat his words out fitfully, in staccato bursts. "I was goin to divide his gear up along with the money, but now I don't think I got any use for it. Any of you guys want any of this stuff, step up and claim it." He looked around him. Nobody moved. "Well, that's somethin anyhow," he said.

He studied Raditzer. "Take those duds off him, Jimmy, just leave him his shorts. This guy ain't walkin off this ship all shined up like the rest of us heroes, I'll tell you that." While Jimmy undressed the body, Hoak shoved Raditzer's effects into the duffel bag, all but the Navy instruments and the Japanese scalp. Jimmy handed him the clothes, and he crammed these after the rest. Standing, he tossed the duffel hard at Big Okie's chest. "You want something overboard so bad, Okie, you throw that overboard." He gave the Navy property to Jimmy, telling him to leave it somewhere near the bridge where it could be found. The scalp he replaced carefully by itself in the paper suitcase and handed the suitcase to Gioncarlo.

"Look, kid," he said uncomfortably, "your name's Gioncarlo—that makes you Catholic, don't it?"

"So what? What are you gettin at, Hoak?" Gioncarlo was very red.

"Don't get excited, kid, I don't mean no harm." He cuffed Gioncarlo gently on the arm. "Look, all I mean is, it just don't seem right to toss this thing over with the slops. You bein a Catholic, you probably got some of the feel of how to do this decent."

"Okay," Gioncarlo said. "Only I want to take care of it alone, my own way."

"You do it any way you want," Hoak said.

Stark, the strength gone out of him, leaned heavily against the bulkhead as the other men, one by one, drifted away down the passageways to their bunks. Slowly he became aware that he was being watched. But only he and Hoak remained in the compartment, and the fat man, smoking a slow cigarette, had his broad, immobile back to him. Turning slightly, Stark thought he saw an eye gleaming in the shadows, and although this seemed impossible, he wondered if Raditzer was conscious, had been conscious all along. Yet the body was perfectly still. A worn sole protruded into the light, and part of the white leg of its beaten, near-naked owner. Unable to see Raditzer's face, Stark turned his head away and felt ashamed.

"What's this guy to you?" Hoak said at last, exhaling a mighty burst of smoke in a sigh that seemed to expend the last of his emotions.

"I don't know," Stark answered wearily, unable to attempt an answer to this question all over again.

"I mean, he ain't much of a guy," Hoak continued. "I don't know as I ever met any man I had less use for so quick, and that's sayin a good deal."

"I know," Stark said.

"Well, I don't know as I like your tastes." Hoak

turned and faced Stark for the first time. "I don't even know as I like you." He laughed shortly, ruefully, grinding out his cigarette beneath his heel. "In fact, for a while there I had you figured for a real yellow-belly, Stark, after you jumped in and started sluggin the little bastard. I knew there was something phony about the way you done it, and I figured you was tryin to save your own skin, see?"

"I guess everybody figured that."

"I guess they did. I guess they still do. One way or another, you ain't made yourself very popular. You don't mind that?"

"Oh, I mind, I suppose." He minded very much, more than he wanted to admit, because never before in his life had he been an outcast. But he minded most about Raditzer, who had seen himself turned upon by the one human being on earth he imagined to be his friend and who would never permit himself to understand.

Hoak nodded. "Well, you stand by what you think, I'll give you that much. You're stickin your neck out in a piss-poor cause, believe me. Still, I'm grateful you did, for Carl and me and the rest." He offered his hand, and Stark took it.

"Let's get him on a sack," Stark said.

"Okay. We don't want him dyin on us of pneumomia after all that trouble, I don't guess." Hoak stepped over to Raditzer and toed him roughly in the ribs. "Get up off the deck," he said. "There ain't nobody goin to carry you."

But Raditzer lay still, and they finally carried him. It was not until they had stretched him on a bunk that he opened his eyes and looked both men in the face with what Stark recognized as impudence. He seemed to know that Stark knew he had been conscious from the start and had indulged him in his need to be carried rather than expose this new duplicity to the anger of Hoak. His expression was blunted, however, by the cuts and shiny swellings of his distorted face, and Stark could not be certain.

Hoak was suspicious too. "You sorry sonofabitch," he said to Raditzer. "I got a notion you was layin awake there all the time."

Raditzer painfully curled his lip and stared straight at the canvas above his head, and this time his contempt for them was unmistakable. His eyes were murderous, and his cut, pulpy mouth clamped tight, as if he meant never to speak again.

"You know something, Raditzer?" Hoak said. "You're goin to lay right there, alone in this compartment, until this ship ties up in San Francisco. You ain't getting out of that there bunk even if you drown in your own piss. You're goin to march off this ship just the way you are now, and you ain't got nothin comin to you in the meantime, you hear that? And you start feeling sorry for yourself, you just keep in mind that you only got this guy here to thank for bein alive at all."

Raditzer slowly turned his head and glared at Stark, then turned away again. Raising his hand to his swollen face, he began an outrageous sniveling, but his eyes remained glittering and tearless.

"Holy God!" Hoak said. "He turns my stomach."

Stark followed Hoak out through the arch into their own compartment. He felt no pity, only anger, directionless and bitter.

"Don't you think you're being a little rough on him?" he said suddenly, sharply. And Hoak stopped.

"No, I don't," Hoak said. "First of all, Stark, though I'm glad it didn't happen now I'm cooled off, I was one of them was ready to throw him over the side—he deserved it."

"Deserved murder? Christ! How can you be so sure?"

"Nobody would call that murder." For one instant Hoak looked uncertain. "It ain't like one guy killin another. I ain't no murderer, Stark." Hoak reached around with one big hand and rubbed the back of his neck. For a moment his tough face was imploring, haunted, and Stark winced for him. "But I mean this Raditzer don't have the right to screw us, not guys been through what some of these guys have. Him and his dirty mouth and his dirty goddam souvenirs and his crap about seein combat—Jesus, he made you wonder why you were out there all them lousy years gettin shot at in the first place, he took all the point out of it, like, he made it seem cheap, see what I mean? I don't know how he did it, but he did."

Stark stood silent.

"Look, Stark, a guy might just be getting by in life, takin care of his own troubles. Then a guy like this Raditzer comes along—he makes it impossible maybe. Well, then it's you or him, that's all. When there ain't no law to take care of him, you got to take care of him yourself, ain't that right?"

"I don't know." Stark sighed. "Look, I'm going to get him a blanket, and some food and water now and then."

Hoak shrugged. "Why not? I'd like to see him walk off this barge under his own power."

"How about roll calls?"

"How many roll calls you heard since the Navy told you, Go on home? The next time we'll get roll call, Stark, is probably in Frisco."

"What makes you think he won't turn us all in?"

"I just don't think he will. He got a good look at Carl there in the beginning, I seen his face, and I just don't think he will. For some reason this Raditzer values his life. And anyway, who's goin to back him up? Who's goin to believe a guy like that or even listen to him?"

But Stark's mind had wandered to something else, to Hoak and Carl, Jimmy and Big Okie, the four of them linked in a nameless destiny by one common episode in their past. Hoak wished to believe they had acted that other time for the good of society, and doubtless society would have contrived to forgive them for the execution of Raditzer as well. But he wondered if Hoak, a good man, would forgive himself for what had happened at Saipan in all the next half-century of his life.

"Oh, yeah," Hoak added, taking a soiled envelope from his hip pocket. "I found this on the floor. It's addressed to Mrs. Charlie Stark, no address." He gazed at Stark. "It's sealed."

Stark took it. "Thanks," he said.

"If he should happen to fall overboard after all," Hoak said sourly, "I might even get to like you."

Stark went up on deck and pieced out the letter by the light of his cigarette.

Dear Charlotte

This is from Rad which is what my buddys call me and please call me too. Probably Charlie already wrote you about us being buddys. I guess he'd say I am his best buddy only I feel like your friend too. Excuse me only its like I love you almost like you was a princess kind of or maybe brotherly love one human bean for another human but nothing dirty. I never felt this way before so please dont laugh. Anyway he dont love you

like he should and cheated on you. Her name is Myrna.
I decided this was my duty to tell you this for your own
good. Maybe you would want to talk to me sometime
after I get home in maybe two weeks. Just write me M.
Raditzer, General Delivery, L.A., and I will be there
day or night. Only dont tell Charlie.

Your secret friend always
Rad

When he was through he let the dawn breeze snap
the paper from his hand. It fluttered away downwind
and stuck on the viscous sea, pale as a face in the dark
gray of first light.

In the hour left him Stark slept badly. He dreamed
of Hiroshima, of a gray skeletal landscape where a
hellish mob, tattered and charred, pursued a screech-
ing Raditzer across the smoking ruins. He himself
was running with the mob, striving to dissuade them,
but he did not run fast enough, and Raditzer was
stoned to earth and lay there dying. He stood over
Raditzer, shouting, He's no guiltier than yourselves!
You're all guilty! And Raditzer, shriveling on a bed
of cinders, whispered, You too! You too! You're no
better than the rest! There came an awful cackle, and
Stark turned to see Charlotte writhing, eyes closed, in
the embrace of a faceless man.

The physical actuality was so strong that he cried

out, and knocked his head as he sat upright in his berth.

He got out Charlotte's recent letters and read them carefully again, trying to find the seed of his uneasiness. The letters struck him more and more as tense and cryptic, and the endearments few and formal. Sinking back in his berth, he tried to imagine how the girl he had known would write to him if she had been unfaithful, and concluded she would write in just this way. In his chest his heart tugged painfully, like a small animal caught in a wire snare.

In the week that followed, the *Pendleton* swept swiftly eastward. Blue days opened one by one and died with the bald sun firing the wake. Oblivious of men and ships, lone albatross and shearwaters carved the silent seas, wings stiff as fins, and porpoises rolled past, and flying fish sprayed outward from the bow wave. The men lying in the sun emerged dazedly from the dark of war and laughed too loudly.

Only Raditzer, prostrate below, was silent. Stark tended to him, tried to talk to him, but Raditzer would not respond. Even one day when Carl had gone up to the foredeck for the afternoon and Stark, unable to bear Raditzer's degradation any longer, had ordered him out of his bunk to clean himself, the man affected not to listen. In Stark's plea lay Raditzer's triumph—his quick eyes betrayed him—but his revenge had just begun. The men, who at first had come singly and in groups to peer in upon the prisoner, now stayed away, repelled less by the squalor of his cell than by the sharing of his shame which his martyrdom forced upon them. Perhaps more than at any other time in a life apparently devoted to this end, Stark thought, Raditzer had compelled his fellow men to face their own frailty as represented in himself. His perversity was boundless, and yet there was something forlorn in his dedication to it which almost redeemed him, after all.

Eight days out of Pearl Harbor the Farallon Islands came in sight, with the coast of California a dim shadow in the distance. The men crowded to the bow rails, all but Raditzer, and all but Raditzer gave a shout of glory an hour later when the *Pendleton* passed beneath the Golden Gate. Raditzer, alone in the yellow glare of his compartment, was blind to the great, proud banners with legends like WELCOME HOME, BOYS, and GOD BLESS YOU FOR A JOB WELL DONE. Such greetings flew everywhere along the bay front, and band music floated gently to their ears. Horns honked and tugboats whistled, and there came a faint, dismal clamor from the island penitentiary of Alcatraz.

The men had taken their gear above decks early in

the morning, and the compartments lay deadly silent. Stark came down a last time as the ship was edged against her pier.

"Come on, Raditzer, let's get you washed. We're home."

But Raditzer said nothing, did not stir, nor did he glance at the clean pair of shorts Stark laid out for him on the next bunk. He simply lay back, hands behind his head, and formed with his still-swollen lips a mute obscenity. To Stark's surprise, however, a tear formed steadily in the corner of Raditzer's eye and trickled down at last across the grimed stubble of his face. Whether it stemmed from self-pity or from some deep, hidden well of grief Stark never knew.

And then quite suddenly, and for the first time in a week, Raditzer spoke. "I seen Myrna the night before I come aboard. She had this abortion. Your kid."

"I don't believe you."

"Well, Charlie-boy, I didn't believe her neither. But she had this abortion, all right, because I checked up on her story with them Chinamen in my place." He hiked himself painfully onto one elbow, studying Stark's face, and his breath was terrible.

"Why should I believe all this? That it was mine?"

Raditzer lay back, sighing out his contempt, and replaced his hands behind his head. "You don't have to believe nothin you don't want to, Charlie boy. That's the story of your life."

Stark seized the man and shook him violently, but a moment later he let go. Raditzer nodded wisely. Stark couldn't bear the sight of Raditzer any longer, and at the same time he knew that the guilt was not Raditzer's, and that he had long ago relinquished, in Raditzer's eyes as well as his own, any claim he might have had to moral outrage. He thought of the aborted child, wiped away by the forces of a society which had no place for it, and wondered what his course would have been had Myrna told him.

We are not animals, after all, his father had once, inaccurately, assured him. *We maintain charities and asylums. Among animals, the old, the weak, are driven out or even killed.*

But there were human parallels, Stark thought. Innocence was no excuse for that ultimate crime against society—less forgivable by far than rape, assault, murder itself—the crime of getting in the way. In his own times, by this criterion, Christ himself was at the very least a famous nuisance.

"You must've got quite a kick out of hittin me that night, huh, Charlie? Imagine me thinkin you was different from the rest!"

"Come on," Stark said. And though he imagined he felt pity, his voice sounded peremptory and cold.

Raditzer cocked his narrow head, teeth bared in a

grin. "Is Charlotte out there?" he said. "Is she?"

"Yes," Stark said. "I suppose she is."

Raditzer's inquiry from this debased position disgusted him, and the will to stifle the man's terrible needs came over him like a fever. To control himself, he thought about the letter. But the pity he had felt on reading it, the understanding he had always wished to feel for Raditzer, had snapped away, laying bare taut hatred. My God, he thought, what's happening to me, what's happening? The very first time he had seen Raditzer, he had seized him up like a dog seizing a rat, and he had to restrain himself from giving way still more violently to that first impulse of horror and distaste, from yanking him to his feet and hurling him headlong from his sight. Whatever else, that impulse had been honest.

You hypocrite, he told himself, you pious hypocrite —but that was the stern old voice of his upbringing, where everything had its moral place, and he was no longer in a mood to listen. He felt a mad, furious elation.

"Come on, Raditzer," he said. "Let's go."

"You ever write her about me, Charlie? Did you?"

"Yes."

"About old Rad bein your pal and all?"

No.

"You turned on me, Charlie," Raditzer muttered when Stark was silent. "You let them whip me like I was a dog or somethin, like I didn't deserve to live."

"You believe what you like," Stark said. "I was trying to help you."

"You and me know better." Raditzer sighed. Turning over onto his stomach, he ran his fingertips across the rivet heads on the floor plates. "You and me," he repeated wistfully, with something like regret. "They whipped me like I was a dog or somethin," he said again after a moment, scarcely audible.

Then he looked up. "You snotty bastard, Charlie." He was crying. "You put up with me because I told you how great you was, but I learnt you ain't no different from the rest. You'd like to see me dead."

"That's right," Stark said quietly. "That's all exactly right. You come near me or my wife ever again, and I'll kill you myself."

"I ain't done with you yet, Stark, you hear that? You hear that, Stark? Where you goin now? Hey, where you goin, Charlie?"

The man's wail, trailing him, ricocheted among the metal rooms. Stark climbed the ladders swiftly. Emotions flew about his head, colliding. He pitched, sun-blinded, out onto the deck.

"Where's your buddy at?" said Steve R. Kubichek. "Ain't he comin?"

"Listen, he's not my—" Charlie stopped. "He didn't tell me."

The men were marched promptly off the *Pendleton,* duffels on their shoulders, and were greeted as they left the gangplank by the civilian crowd assembled behind a barrier under the great shed of the pier. The band music broke out, "El Capitan," and American mothers in white smocks passed up and down the ranks, dispensing coffee. The men, standing at ease, talked animatedly among themselves. They were overexcited and a little selfconscious, especially those who, like Stark, felt themselves impostors among the battle veterans. Gioncarlo, whom Hoak and his friends had adopted as a sort of mascot, was arranging with these men a later meeting in a bar on the Embarcadero, and Stark realized that he himself was not going to be invited.

The man named Carl stood a little apart, as he always did. He was preoccupied and unsmiling, apparently oblivious of the sights and sounds. Nevertheless his face was more open to the world than it had been even eight days before, and his bayonet had been dropped without ceremony over the side as the Farallons passed astern, joining, in the deeps of the Pacific, Raditzer's accumulation of gewgaws and the black-haired memento of Armageddon consecrated to the sea by Gioncarlo.

Quietly, across the din, Hoak said to Charlie Stark, "How is he?" and Stark shrugged. "I left him a clean pair of shorts," he said. Hoak shrugged, relapsing once more into his own thoughts.

Stark gazed intently into the crowd and felt unaccountably shy. At last he located Charlotte, flanked by her parents, his parents—why had she brought them?—and the little group seemed terribly remote, judgmental, like an old-fashioned family portrait on a wall. In the next instant it was clear to him that Charlotte was there under duress and that she had been crying. He thought of her last letters, and he thought of Raditzer.

Now you take with Charlotte, love is a thing of beauty, like, kind of a joy forevermore, you might say. She wouldn't cheat on you, huh, Charlie?

And he knew as surely as a man knows he is dying that their future would be at best that compromise with life which, like death itself, happened only to other people.

For the moment, stunned, he pretended to search the crowd for these people he could not bear to see, letting his blind gaze stare past them. The voice of the crowd was lost in the remote stir of the great city. Time hung suspended. Then the dizziness went, and he heard Charlotte's voice calling from far away, out of the past.

He turned in time to see her broken smile. Uneasily, the others waved, and his hand rose vaguely in response.

The ship's company, its duty done, had disappeared below or drifted to the taffrail aft to contemplate the crowd. The rails and the gangplank head were clear, and a solitary gull, bright white against the blue, commandeered the bow. It turned its head, and its yellow beak gleamed cruelly in the sun. Stark fidgeted. Behind the impassive hull casting its shadow on the pier, the exiled Raditzer would trail the echoes upward through the empty troop holds of a finished war, his bare feet dank on the tired metal. Perhaps he was already crouched above their heads, on that altar of steel and sky, spying down on his tormentors.

A roll call was taken, and Raditzer was discovered missing. The coxswain in charge of their company asked if anybody had seen him, and, when nobody answered, demanded in exasperation whether this Raditzer had friends. The men looked pointedly at Stark, and Stark said nothing.

"The list here says this Raditzer is aboard the *Pendleton*," the coxswain snapped. "So far as I'm concerned, he's still aboard, and you men ain't leavin this pier without him." He shouted up at one of the

Pendleton's crew to have Raditzer's name called on the public address system.

"Who?" The crewman had just that minute lounged against the boat deck rail and was plainly annoyed at having to move.

"RA-ditzer!"

"RAD-zinger?" Sloppy and unshaven, the man heaved sulkily from the rail, taking his time as pointedly as possible.

Then the coxswain faced the men, belligerent. They were silent, and the crowd fell silent too. "We're goin to search the ship," the coxswain said, "and this here company is goin to stand at attention until we find him. Atten-*tion!*"

Slowly the men straightened, brought their heels together. A few glared openly at Stark. Then there was quiet. The coxswain looked over their faces, affecting a steely eye. "All right," he said, "who knows this man?"

"I know him," Stark said.

"Well, step out here then, goddam it! Who else?"

Gioncarlo and then Hoak came forward and stood at attention beside Stark.

"All right," the coxswain said, "go get him. And get him quick, or you'll all explain it to the shore patrol."

But the order was unnecessary. A woman in the crowd gave a little squeal, lost immediately in a general gasp. Raditzer, dressed only in the clean shorts too big for him, was standing at the head of the gangplank. His body shrunk against the sky, he looked like a boy awakened out of sleep, confused and vulnerable.

On the bow the gull shifted uneasily and blinked.

"All right, come down off there!" the coxswain shouted. "You're under arrest!"

Raditzer crawled up onto the iron rails and rose precariously to his feet. The American flag flew proudly overhead. Teetering, he gave the flag a wild, obscene salute, once, twice, three times, and the crowd gasped again. The gasp changed to a groan of disapproval, and individual voices leaped up above the rest—*Didja see what he done to the flag? Didja?— What's he tryna do, commit suicide?—*

He ain't even dressed decent, a woman's voice said, and another woman's voice cried out to Raditzer, *You gonna insult Old Glory, then whyncha jump?* And a man's voice, a stadium voice, roared, *G'wan, ya dirty bum, ya! Jump!*

Stark ran forward, and the coxswain shouted at him. Above his head Raditzer swayed, black as a flying cinder against the high blaze of noon.

"Raditzer!" Stark called. "Hey, Rad!"

And Raditzer, startled, whirled to peer down at him, watching Stark's face avidly even as his own mouth popped open in alarm. For he had lost his balance. Though his feet clung for a moment, he was falling. He screamed, "Charlie!" His body revolved once slowly inexorably, like a moon, in that rigid second of hallucination before his head struck the piling. The impact threw his arms apart, spread-eagling him in the air, and it seemed to Stark that he remained suspended in this way for a split second before dropping to the pier edge. The body slammed over in a half-revolution and poised an instant on its side. Then it disappeared, its splash into the water inaudible.

The voice of the crowd, wrenched from it by the fall like a hoarse, mighty cough of laughter, died to silence.

At the edge of the pier, Stark fell upon his knees. There was no sign of Raditzer. The ship's hull gleamed where the splash had wet it, but the water had closed and turned peacefully in the tide. A grapefruit rind revolved in the slit between hull and pilings before the current swept it out of sight into the labyrinths beneath the pier. Near the submerged posts the minnows poised, quick as thin magnets, and far below an eel swayed in the green sea algaes clinging to the creosoted wood.

Still kneeling, Stark half-turned to face the crowd. He stared at it in disbelief, his arms limp at his sides. Is that what you wanted, he wondered. Is that what I really wanted? The faces stared back in the shocked stillness—as if I were the murderer, he thought. Am I? How unreal and silent the world seemed. On his knees before these people, in the bright sun of the arena, he felt himself irretrievably cut off, alone.

The coxswain had run forward. "All right," his voice said, "get back in ranks. You're on report." He kneeled and stared angrily into the water. "Holy Christ." He stood up again. "What's the matter with you, sailor? Get the hell back in ranks!" Stark did not move. On the bridge over their heads the great loudspeaker crackled, snapped, and a bored voice, arguing with someone in the background, blew into it and spoke.

choufa choufa.

Now hear this

Rad—

wheep **How do** ping **pernounce that**

snap **Jesus** snap

work this goddam thing?

ratchety ratchety ping

Rad-zinger ping

Report immediately to the snarak chouf chouf

on the double, sailor

Stark sat down hard on the pier. Blood spatter gleamed on the dry gray-splintered wood, and he felt sick.

Raditzer's dead. We killed him.

His own words sounded very far away to him, he could scarcely hear them. He banged the side of his head with the flat of his hand.

"Take it easy. Take it easy, now, Charlie. It was an accident." Jack's voice, beating at Stark's awareness like wings at a glass pane, sounded close to tears. Jack was pale as paper.

"*It* was *an accident, Charlie.*" Hoak's voice came quietly from somewhere, remorseless as water over stone. "That's the way life goes, you hear me, Charlie?"

Repeat   Rad-zinger

wheedle—ee—yip crack   **This motherf**

Stark frowned. He shook his head violently, as if drunk. *I killed him,* his own voice said. Then he heard somebody laughing—was it himself?—and then his face was slapped. Hoak's eyes snapped into place in front of him, and reality returned with a great rush and roar.

"All right," the coxswain shouted, "I ain't goin to tell you again—get that man back in ranks!"

Hoak loomed over him, pores sharp as bullet holes in his swart face. "Now you ain't no murderer, Charlie, ain't none of us murderers, so it's got to be a accident." He squatted in front of him so that they faced each other, commanding attention with talons tight on Charlie's shoulders. "You listen to me, now. There's goin to be questions. You go sayin anybody killed that man, we're goin to say you ain't in your right mind about it, that no such a thing never happened."

The hint of threat was present in Hoak's voice—if you are guilty of that man's death, then so are we, and we won't acknowledge that.

"The rest of us are goin to testify against you."

Hoak awaited Stark without expression, and Stark stood. He was unsteady on his feet, and when he tried to turn away from them, Hoak caught him. He took Stark's face between his hands as if shaping it in clay.

"Forget it," Hoak said.

"Forget it," Hoak said.

Forget it.

He took Stark's arm and, preceded by Gioncarlo, started him in the direction of the ranks.

An officer and two shore patrolmen with yellow arm brassards came trotting up. They kneeled to look under the pier. When they got up they shook their heads at the coxswain. All four wore battle ribbons. The officer said something, and one of the patrolmen grinned uneasily. Less hurriedly now, they crossed through the crowd to the far side of the pier, where they looked at the water without bothering to kneel.

Still clutching their flags, the spectators observed them, and the men in ranks stirred restlessly, watching Stark. His legs were stiff as stilts, and he had stopped. He stared vacantly at the harbor, where an excursion boat, passing the *Pendleton*'s slip, hooted a greeting at the sailors.

A car horn, a drone of summer planes, a foolish tooting from afar. Heat shimmered on the oiled planking of the pier. The sun rode high, the banners flew, and on a stand draped with bunting of red, white, and blue the bandleader, deaf to any sound but his own music, whirled away into "The Stars and Stripes Forever."

Repeat   wheep wheep
wheedle-o

When Hoak nudged him, he started up again. Before his eyes swam the line of Gioncarlo's haircut, fresh and raw, and he recalled with a loose, sudden smile that Jack's girl was in the crowd. Jack had reached up and cocked his cap upon his brow, walking ahead selfconsciously, like an athlete.

On the bow of the ship the gull stretched its dry leg and wing, then slipped forward and glided out across the harbor. The faces of Charlotte and his family, in the front row, stared at Stark. He took his place in line.

ABOUT THE AUTHOR

Peter Matthiessen was born in New York City in 1927 and had already begun his writing career by the time he graduated from Yale University in 1950. The following year, he was a founder of *The Paris Review*. Besides *At Play in the Fields of the Lord*, which was nominated for the National Book Award, he has published four other novels, including *Far Tortuga*. Mr. Matthiessen's unique career as a naturalist and explorer has resulted in numerous and widely acclaimed books of nonfiction, among them *The Tree Where Man Was Born* (with Eliot Porter), which was nominated for the National Book Award, and *The Snow Leopard*, which won it. His other works of nonfiction include *The Cloud Forest* and *Under the Mountain Wall* (which together received an Award of Merit from the National Institute of Arts and Letters), *The Wind Birds, Blue Meridian, Sand Rivers, In the Spirit of Crazy Horse, Indian Country,* and, most recently, *Men's Lives*. His novel-in-progress and a collection of his short stories will be published by Random House.